SUNSET RANCH

flirt

Read the Entire Flirt Series!

SUNSET RANCH

A. Destiny and Emma Carlson Berne

SIMON PULSE

NEW YORK   LONDON   TORONTO   SYDNEY   NEW DELHI

SIMON PULSE

An imprint of Simon & Schuster Children's Publishing Division

1230 Avenue of the Americas, New York, NY 10020

This Simon Pulse edition August 2015

Text copyright © 2014 by Simon & Schuster, Inc.

Cover photograph copyright © 2015 by Phillip Lee Harvey/Getty Images

All rights reserved, including the right of reproduction in whole or in part in any form.

SIMON PULSE and colophon are registered trademarks of Simon & Schuster, Inc.

For information about special discounts for bulk purchases, please contact Simon & Schuster Special Sales at 1-866-506-1949 or business@simonandschuster.com.

The Simon & Schuster Speakers Bureau can bring authors to your live event. For more information or to book an event contact the Simon & Schuster Speakers Bureau at 1-866-248-3049 or visit our website at www.simonspeakers.com.

Designed by Regina Flath

The text of this book was set in Adobe Caslon Pro.

Manufactured in the United States of America

10 9 8 7 6 5 4 3 2 1

Library of Congress Control Number 2014936616

ISBN 978-1-4814-5189-5 (pbk)

ISBN 978-1-4424-8411-5 (eBook)

Chapter ● One

hitched my backpack higher onto my shoulders and brushed back my hair, which already felt ickily greasy. My flight out of Cincinnati had left at six a.m., so I'd skipped a shower. My guitar case seemed to weigh a thousand pounds, and I was beginning to question the wisdom of hauling it all the way out here. As I made my way toward the baggage claim through the cavernous, glass-ceilinged terminal, I tried not to stare as men in actual cowboy hats and boots strode by. Air force soldiers in sleek navy uniforms shouldered big blue duffels. Families with long zippered ski bags struggled past. Out the huge picture windows the mountains hulked, white and blue-gray against an impossibly azure sky. I shivered a little and grinned to myself—this was really Colorado. I was really here, thousands of miles from home, for three months. I wanted to sing my way down the terminal.

I followed the river of people out of the main terminal, stepped onto a down escalator, followed a long underground passage to an up escalator, then allowed myself to be swept along to another up escalator. I was wondering just how much longer I'd be trailing around this airport when the escalator deposited me in front of several baggage carousels.

I hurried over to the nearest one and scanned the conveyor belt for my khaki-green army surplus duffel. Mom had been so proud when she found it for only five dollars at the thrift store. There it was, riding around and around, looking like an abandoned stuffed animal in the midst of all the black rolling suitcases surrounding it. I elbowed through a scrum of random passengers and reached forward, managing to snag the strap just as the bag moved past. Puffing slightly, I dragged it toward me and let it thump to the floor.

"Hey, thanks for getting my bag," someone said in a southern drawl.

I looked up into the clearest blue eyes I'd ever seen.

A tall boy about my own age was standing beside me. He had a backpack too, and he wore a gray T-shirt that read PACIFIC FOOD CO-OP and frayed khaki shorts with sandals. His black hair fell over his forehead, and his eyes were startlingly light against his tanned skin. He smiled, showing sparkling white teeth. A leather band circled one broad wrist and a narrow silver chain glinted under the collar of his T-shirt.

I closed my mouth, which had fallen open slightly, and cleared my throat. "Ah, sorry. This is my bag." I tried to sound cute and casual, though I think it came out sounding more strained and weird.

He didn't even blink. "It was probably a long flight, huh? You're just a little confused." He flashed me another grin and looped his hand under the strap. "Anyway, like I said, thanks for getting it for me. See you around."

"Hey!" It came out louder than I intended, and several people turned to look. "Excuse me! I don't know who you are, but that's *my* bag. Put it down. Please."

The boy studied the duffel, looked at me for such a long moment that I flushed, then looked back at the duffel again. A slow grin spread across his face. "Let's see. My bag was my dad's, from the army. So *if* you're telling the truth, why would you have the same kind of bag? Unless you're in the army yourself." He was teasing me—that much was clear. I wondered if my neck was going all splotchy.

"I'm not in the army. My mom got it at the army surplus store. Okay?" I swiped at the bag, but he slid it back out of my reach and shook his head.

"No way. I can spot a solider a mile away. What's your rank?"

I had to laugh. "I'm not exactly the military type—can't you tell?"

He let his gaze slowly wander from my feet to my head. "No way. You're tough. I mean, look at those muscles." He squeezed my upper arm, and my pulse shot up. "Come on, what do you bench?"

I rolled my eyes. "Very funny. Look, can I *please* have my bag?"

"Hmm. I say it's mine; you say it's yours. What should we do?" His eyes crinkled up at the edges, and a dimple appeared in his left cheek as his smile deepened. For one electric instant we looked into each other's eyes. Then I cut my gaze away, thoroughly rattled.

"Here." I grabbed the zipper and pulled. The bag fell open, revealing several pairs of purple and pink underwear lying on the top of a mound of jeans and T-shirts. *Oops.*

The boy laughed out loud, the sound echoing in the big room. "Hey, I can't argue with that. Are those standard military issue?"

My cheeks flamed. Of course I'd forgotten the underwear was on the top. I struggled with the zipper, but a pair of the underwear was caught in the teeth. Now I had no desire for anything but to get away from this person as fast as I could. "You're funny, I can see that. Hilarious, actually." I yanked at the zipper again.

"It's one of my special talents. Here, let me." The boy pulled hard at the zipper and raked it up to the top.

I exhaled. "Thanks. Anyway. Nice to meet you." A little trickle of sweat ran down my chest, but at least my underwear was safely out of sight again. Without looking at him, I grabbed my bag and marched away toward the glass exit doors.

"Hey, what's your name?" he called after me.

"Private McKinley," I yelled back over my shoulder. Then, just as I turned around again—*bam*. I slammed into the clear glass door.

"Ooh," I moaned, holding my forehead, letting my bag slide from my shoulder. Something dripped from my fingers, and I looked down to see bright blood splotching the floor at my feet.

"Was that on purpose, Private McKinley?" The guy was suddenly beside me, prying my fingers from my numb face. He smelled like peppermint gum. "Because it's cool about the suitcase and all. You don't have to bleed to make a point."

"I'm fine," I managed, trying to wipe my face but succeeding only in smearing the blood. "Okay? Thanks for your help. This happens to me all the time."

"Nice. Have you ever considered a helmet?" The guy was waving at one of the airport security guards, who came hurrying over.

"Oh now, miss, why don't you come with me to first aid?" The burly man was leaning over me. Then a ticket agent appeared, holding a towel.

"Poor little girl! We have to get you downstairs. . . ."

Another agent strode over. "She might need stitches. . . ."

I pressed the white towel to my brow and looked around. The boy was gone.

Chapter ☙ Two

A half hour later I stood at the curb just outside the terminal, army bag and guitar in hand, watching the varicolored airport vans and shuttles slide by. My right eyebrow was neatly plastered with a white butterfly bandage applied by the nice medic in the first aid office. I'd managed to get most of the blood off my face by scrubbing with paper towels in the bathroom, though some stubborn specks still remained crusted by my hairline.

I craned my neck to look down the long line of waiting vehicles. The last e-mail from the ranch had said someone would pick me up soon after my flight. Had my ride come and gone while I was getting my face patched up?

I took out my phone and thumbed through my e-mail until I found the acceptance note.

Dear Chloe,

We are pleased to offer you a position as a summer worker at the Nickel River Dude Ranch. As a stable hand, your duties will entail daily horse feeding, grooming, and turnout, assisting guests and riding instructors as needed, accompanying guests and staff on ranch outings and trail rides, cleaning and organizing tack, and other duties as assigned. Expect long days, hard work, and a lot of fun. Please bring ...

Etc., etc.

Every Saturday since I was ten years old, I would take the number 78 bus up Springfield Pike, right on Fleming, left on Winton, fifteen minutes, staring out the window as the bus jerked and puffed past genteel houses on big wooded lots, me and all the women clutching plastic grocery bags and the men in flannel shirts bound for shifts at the lighting factory just behind the tiny, one-runway airport. The houses disappeared by the top of Fleming, replaced first by fast-food restaurants and big churches and then with garden centers and then the big red-and-white sign looming: WINTON WOODS RIDING CENTER and the little icons below it—a person hiking, a person in a boat, and a person on a horse.

I'd spend the whole day up there, drunk with the smell and

sight of horses—the pungent hay-leather-manure scent of their fur; their big, liquid eyes; the creak and slap of leather as I tacked them up for the lessons and trail rides. I didn't even mind leading the little Shetland pony around and around in circles in the August sun, a four-year-old clutching the saddle horn and speechless with terror and delight.

I saw a rusted green pickup chugging at the curb in front of me. I stuffed my phone in my pocket and ran toward it as an auburn-haired boy in a worn plaid shirt jumped from the driver's seat. "Hey, are you Chloe?" he called.

I stopped, trying not to stare. "Yeah, hi," I managed to reply.

His eyes crinkled up at the corners when he smiled. That always just kills me. "Stephen. I'm your ride—and your coworker."

Thank you. Thank you, God.

Stephen lifted my bag from my shoulder and tossed it into the bed of the truck as if it were stuffed with tissues instead of three months worth of every outfit I thought I might need. "Hey, a guitar! Do you play?"

"Just a little. I goof around on it."

He extended a sunburned hand to help me into the truck. "What happened to your eye?"

Up close, I could see the freckles smattered across his nose and the tops of his cheeks. His tousled hair glinted red-gold with thick strands curling over the back of his collar. I was gaping, I realized. I think he did too, because his eyes met mine for a searching instant. I looked away and giggled nervously.

"Um, my eye?" I touched the butterfly with one finger. I was about to come out with some lie about tripping when I got off the plane, but something in his face stopped me. "You really want to know? I ran my face into a glass door."

"I did that once! At an art museum. My cousin told me I left a big face print on the glass."

We both laughed, and I climbed onto the rough, dog-hair-covered front seat of the pickup. Stuffing boiled up like popcorn from rips in the upholstery, and the footwell was scattered with a liberal assortment of hay, smashed grain, and pop cans. I exhaled and leaned back against the seat as Stephen slammed the driver's door.

"Sorry about the mess," he said, leaning over and trying to clear away a little of the debris.

"No, it's great. I love it, actually."

He looked at me as if I'd told him I was actually the Duchess of Cambridge. "Seriously? The window doesn't even roll up. Most girls wouldn't like that."

I raised my eyebrows at him. "Maybe I'm not like most girls."

He grinned. "Maybe . . ." He glanced toward the terminal. "By the way, we're just waiting for one other hand too."

"Okay, no problem." I smiled at him. "So, how long have you worked at Nickel River?"

Stephen leaned back and traced a circle around the wheel. "Three years now. My brother's the trainer there. I come out during the summers to help him. Hopefully, I'll be assistant trainer one of these days." A shadow passed over his face, too quick for me to read.

"I've never been on a ranch before," I confessed, watching some kind of sports team stream from the airport doors. Football, I guessed from the size of the bags. "I've just worked at this stable near my house."

"Well, don't worry, it's not like roping cows or anything. The wranglers take care of the real cowboy stuff." His eyes were the color of the sea glass I used to pick up on the beach in Maine. "The guy who runs it, Jack, is kind of one of those gruff cowboy types, but really nice underneath. There's about fifty horses in the herd and some goats and some random chickens. The whole place is about eight hundred acres."

"Oh my God, that sounds amazing!" I clapped my hands together in excitement. "I can't wait to see it. Do we get to feed the goats?"

He laughed a little. "Why? Do you have a fetish about goats?"

"I love goats! We couldn't have them at my stable back home because they can get out of any fence. We used to keep one, and she kept escaping and wandering down to the main road. Once, she made it all the way to the Kroger and ate a bunch of tomatoes in the outside display before they caught her."

Stephen guffawed. "Nice! Our nanny goat is kind of old and fat, so she's not going anywhere. But there's lots of wildlife. These black bears like to get into the trash cans, and there's a big herd of antelope you can see from this one overlook."

"Oh, antelope! I've never seen any. Are they like deer?"

"Yeah, except prettier. I'll take you up there sometime." He sounded casual, but the tips of his ears turned adorably pink.

"I'd like that." We smiled at each other. Then I saw his eyes shift to something behind me. "There's the other guy."

I turned around to see the black-haired guy from baggage claim climbing into the cab just behind me. Color zoomed up my face to my hairline. "Hi," I croaked.

The boy shoved a green army bag identical to mine into the footwell and leaned over the front seat, extending his hand. "What's up? I'm Zach."

"Nice to meet you, man." Stephen shook his hand.

"I think we've already been introduced." Zach grinned at me. "Private McKinley."

Stephen looked puzzled. "What?"

"Nothing! Just a dumb joke." I eyed Zach, who winked. "I'm Chloe. McKinley."

Stephen looked from me to Zach and back again. "You guys know each other?"

"In a manner of speaking." I pulled the stiff old seat belt across my chest. "Zach was there when I got acquainted with the glass door."

"We had a nice chat about the military," Zach put in from behind us.

Stephen signaled and pulled into the stream of traffic leaving the terminal. "I'm so confused." He accelerated onto a feeder road near the highway. "By the way, it's only about half an hour to the ranch. That's like five minutes out here."

The wind whipped through the cab as we picked up speed, and I sighed and settled back against the seat. The outlying buildings near the airport receded quickly, giving way to flat, dry land splotched with sagebrush and hillocks of yellow grass. Here and there, rickety wooden and wire fences traced their uncertain way across the landscape. And over everything the vast bulk of the mountains—cool, blue giants looming in the distance. Snow like sugar capped their tops, trailing long fingers down the ridged sides. The sun burned a hot hole in the azure sky, but the breeze raised goose bumps on my arms. I had a sense of space upon space, moving through clean, endless layers of air. If I just reached out my hand, I could touch the mountains through the windshield. They were so close—the truck bumped over a pothole and the mountains receded to their proper place. I shook my head. The altitude must be getting to me.

I inhaled deeply, and the thin, hay-scented air tingled my nose. "Cincinnati never smells like this!"

"Is that where you're from?" Stephen asked. He drove easily, one elbow cocked out the window. "I've never been there. My family's all from Denver."

"You're not missing much. It's pretty basic suburban life." I gazed at his profile from under my eyelashes as he drove.

"Where are you from, Zach?" Stephen asked, twisting around slightly.

"Charleston, South Carolina, born and raised," he drawled.

So that was the accent. A Charleston boy. Images of plantation houses with swirling white steps and frostings of wrought iron rose in my mind. Hoop skirts, grits, segregation? "How come you're all the way out here? Don't they have horses closer to Charleston?"

I meant to be funny, of course, and someone could have asked me the same question, but there was only silence from the backseat. I turned around. Zach was looking fixedly out his window, plucking at the torn seat lining with one hand. I had the sense he was deliberately avoiding my gaze.

The silence stretched out until it became awkward. I cast around for something to say. "What—er—what are those rocks?" I pointed to some red giants near the side of the road.

"That's Garden of the Gods," Stephen said. The big rocks were sticking up from stands of pine, softly rounded and smoothed as if carved by the wind. They glowed a soft red-orange in the midafternoon sun. "It's a great place for hiking—we go out there sometimes on our day off."

"We sometimes go down to Red River Gorge in Kentucky to camp, but there's nothing as pretty as that. They have hoedowns every Saturday night—my dad loves those."

"What's a hoedown?" Zach asked from the backseat. I twisted around and cast him a quick glance. He looked totally normal again, with his arm thrown across the back of the seat and one ankle crossed over his knee. Whatever weirdness there was had passed.

"It's like clogging," I explained. Now they both looked confused.

13

"You know, like tap dancing, except kind of country." I mimed twanging a banjo. "With bluegrass music."

"Oh, right." Stephen's brow cleared. "Like *Deliverance*."

A tiny ping of annoyance ran through me. That's what everyone thought of when you started talking about Kentucky or West Virginia. "It's actually not just all hillbillies and moonshine down there." It came out a little sharper than I intended.

"I'm sorry," Stephen said right away. "That was dumb. I should know—everyone thinks all of us in Colorado are either cowboys, gold miners, or ski bums."

"And all of us in Charleston are either hicks or slave-owning, racist snobs," Zach put in.

I snorted. "Actually, I have to confess—I always think of cowboys when I think of Colorado and *Gone with the Wind* when I think of the South." I covered my face with my hands in mock shame and the boys laughed. "I'm so bad."

Stephen braked suddenly as a strange little animal toddled onto the pavement in front of us. It was covered with some kind of armorlike skin and looked like a cross between a pig and a rat.

"Armadillos. They're everywhere out here." Stephen braked and we watched the armadillo snuffle its way across the pavement and disappear into the rough underbrush. "They crash around in the bushes and sound just like a person. It can freak you out to see this little guy wander out instead."

We passed a shuttered gas station, then a few deerlike animals bounding in the grass. Stephen turned off the highway and onto a small side road. The asphalt unspooled before us, broken only by the dotted yellow line in the middle. We were leaving the dry sagebrush country behind, and now slender trees with soft white bark lined the road on either side—aspens, I thought. Grass grew underneath, soft as a carpet, the sun flickering through the cool leaves.

Then the aspens were behind us and waves of grass spread out all around, deep golden, russet, dark green, rustling endlessly in the wind, the colors a stark, almost jarring, contrast to the jewel-blue sky. I rolled down the window the rest of the way. "Is this the prairie?" That sounded very Laura Ingalls Wilder.

"I guess it used to be." Stephen slowed. "It's ranchland now. Here we are."

Two tall pine poles supported a wooden arch with NICKEL RIVER RANCH painted on it in bold white letters. Tubs of bright red flowers were on either side of the narrow gravel drive. I sat up straight, leaning forward as the rocks sprayed from under the truck wheels. We passed a few buildings, all of dark brown wood, set far apart and close to the ground, as if they were huddling from the wind that whipped straight and strong over everything. On either side, chestnut, white, and gray horses grazed in knee-deep pastures behind the wire-and-post fences, their manes and tails fluttering. I couldn't take my eyes off them. A couple of Appaloosas lifted their heads as the truck passed, then ran along beside us, easily keeping up.

"Oh, look!" I breathed. The animals ran as gracefully as music, their legs barely seeming to touch the earth, chins high and muscles rippling, white and brown manes streaming out behind them. "It's like they could keep going forever."

"That's Mickey and Jim," Stephen explained. "They think they're dogs—chase every car that comes onto the place, even ours." He pointed. "There's the ranch house. I'll just drop you guys off—I'm supposed to park in the back."

He stopped the truck and I shoved open my door and climbed down. The wind smacked me full in the face, whipping my long hair behind me—twisting it into unmanageable dreadlocks, no doubt. Behind me, Zach jumped out of the backseat, easily shouldering his bag. Stephen handed me my duffel, then waved and drove off around the building.

A low-slung house of the same brown boards I'd seen in the pasture stood before us, painted with cheerful red trim that matched the bright red rockers on the broad porch. Another low building with double doors, which I guessed was the stable, stood a short distance away, and various other outbuildings stood scattered around. A big yellow dog lying in the shade of the porch lifted its head as we approached and regarded us sleepily, its black nose sniffing the air.

The door opened and a powerfully built, white-haired man stepped out on the porch, wiping his hands on a blue bandanna, which he then stuck in his pocket. "Welcome to Colorado!" he boomed. "How was your trip?" He tramped down the steps and offered his hand, which felt like a piece of leather gear. "I'm Jack,

16

the owner of this place." His face was rough and deeply lined, and his sharp eyes were surrounded by webs of wrinkles. His fingernails were neatly trimmed but rimmed with black, as if he'd been working on an engine. Corded forearms showed beneath the rolled-up cuffs of his denim shirt.

"Chloe." I felt suddenly shy, like I always did in front of big, hearty men.

"Hurt yourself there?" He was looking at my bandaged forehead.

"Er—"

"She had an interview with a door," Zach volunteered, grinning merrily at me.

I resisted the urge to kick Zach in the ankle. "I'm fine now," I said hastily. It would be just my luck if my new boss thought I was a klutz within five minutes of meeting me.

Jack's eyebrows lifted as he looked from me to Zach and back again. "Ah. Well. Let's get you all settled. Zach, why don't you come with me? I'll show you around, and we'll leave Chloe with Stephen."

Thank you, Jack. Thank you very much. Stephen appeared around the side of the house, looking like a red-haired, windblown Adonis. His plaid shirt clung to his broad shoulders, and he walked with a long, easy stride.

Shouldering his duffel again, Zach followed Jack off the porch. "See you later, Private," he called over his shoulder.

I rolled my eyes and focused on Stephen. "Are you going

to show me around?" I asked in what I hoped was a casually flirtatious way.

"Sure." He hoisted my bag onto the porch. "We can just leave that for a bit. We'll do the outside first; then I'll show you the bunkhouse."

He led me around the side of the house. Following him, I admired the way his bulky shoulders stretched his shirt. He wore jeans that were skinnier than the ones guys at home wore, and scuffed, dusty cowboy boots, the kind that looked like he actually rode horses in them.

Stephen stopped in front of the long stable. The big doors were propped open. "So, this is the stable for our section of the ranch. We've got about twenty-five horses in our herd, and the others are pastured in the western and northern sections." He gestured to the prairie, and in the distance I spotted two other clusters of dark-brown buildings huddling low to the ground.

"Oh right, that's where the other guests are?" I remembered back to the information packet they'd sent in the spring. The ranch was divided into three sections, each with its own staff and living quarters and five to ten guests. "How many people are staying right now?" I asked as we wandered down the long empty aisle of stalls.

"Um, let's see." He crinkled up his forehead. "There's the Taylors—parents and two little girls. The kids are kind of crazy. And a lady, Mrs. Coleman. Her husband just died, and this is her first trip without him."

"Oh, that's so sad! What happened to him?"

"Heart attack. He was playing basketball and just fell over."

I winced and he nodded in sympathy. "It seems really rough for her. She cries all the time. Sandra—she's Jack's wife—gave her the best room to kind of help her along. All the guests just got here yesterday—you and Zach are the last staff to arrive."

We walked out the other end of the stable, and Stephen led the way to a little cluster of cabins situated prettily in an aspen grove away from the other buildings. On the porch of one, a young dark-haired woman was reading a book while two snarly-haired little girls whacked each other with sticks. "So, what do we have to do with them?" I asked. "Like, bring them drinks on a tray?" I kept my voice low, though we were far enough away that the woman couldn't possibly have heard us.

"Nah, nothing like that. They have their own little section back here. Mostly, you and I will be working with the horses, and Dana will too. She's the only girl wrangler. I think you're rooming with her. The rest of the wranglers have their own bunkhouse." We wandered away from the guest cabins toward the vast pasture lined with acres of fencing. The wind whipped my hair, bringing the faint scent of snow and pine from the mountains. "It's mostly cleaning stalls, feeding and grooming, tacking up for trail rides, and going along to ride when we need extra help. Dana and Rick—he's my older brother—do most of the heavy horse stuff, like helping the guests, teaching them lessons, leading the rides. Training up new horses." He sighed a little.

"What is it?"

"Huh?" He looked down at me. "Oh. Nothing. It's just—my brother." A corner of his mouth quirked up. "I've been doing the trail-ride-stall-cleaning-horse-care job for three summers now. He keeps saying he'll promote me to assistant trainer once I show him I'm ready." He stared across the pasture as I studied his perfect profile. "I just don't know if he'll ever think I'm ready."

We leaned our arms on the fence, and I gazed at the horses grazing peacefully in the sun, the mountains forming an impossibly beautiful backdrop. The breeze lifted their manes and carried over the faint sound of contented chewing. This was it. I was really here, looking at the mountains, an amazingly nice and cute boy right beside me. A whole summer of horses ahead.

"So, have you ever been away for the summer before?" Stephen asked. He bent down and snapped off a long grass stem, then hopped up on the top fence rail. Leaning over, he extended a hand to me. I grasped his warm, rough fingers and pulled myself up to sit beside him. I balanced on the rail, bracing with my sneakered feet. We were sitting close enough that our arms just brushed.

"No," I confessed. "I usually stay home. Last summer I worked at this diner near our house. I had to wear pantyhose and these orthopedic shoes—they even told us exactly what kind to buy. They looked like my grandma's."

Stephen laughed. "God, I'm sorry."

"Did you ever go to camp?" I ran my fingertips back and forth along the splintery wood of the fence, the sun hot on the top of my head.

He nodded. "Yeah, I used to. My parents sent me to this farm camp when I was nine, and I'd never slept away from home before, except for sleepovers at my friends'. Anyway, this place was run by these farmers who weren't Amish but basically lived like they were. So there wasn't any electricity or plumbing— there was an outhouse made of wood, and every time you used it, you threw in a handful of sawdust from this big bucket when you were done."

"No way!"

"Yes, seriously. And they had all these adopted kids from different countries, and when you got there, some of the teenagers would go through your bag and take out anything you weren't supposed to have." He smiled a little at the memory, as if seeing his nine-year-old self standing in front of him. "And I'd had some problems with bees—I'd been stung and they weren't sure if I was allergic to bees or not. But either way, I had to take Benadryl every six hours, including the middle of the night. So my mom had given me a little alarm clock so I could set it and wake up to take my medicine." He paused.

"And?" I prompted.

He sighed and looked down at his knees. "And one of the teenage kids, who was Russian, I think, and didn't speak much English, found the alarm clock when he was going through my bag and took it away and I started crying. . . ." He looked sheepish at the memory.

It was hard for me to balance this big, square-jawed guy next to me with the small, scared boy in the story. "They shouldn't have been so mean about taking your stuff away."

He grinned. "I know, right? Can you see I'm still scarred?" He hopped down from the fence. "Come on, I'll show you the rest of the place."

At the main house, Stephen caught up my duffel bag from the porch and pushed open the screen door. "So, this is where we eat, hang out, everything." We stepped into a large room, dusky and cool after the outdoors. An old wooden table with benches was pushed in the middle and a series of squashy old couches lined the walls. There was a staircase at either end. I glimpsed a kitchen through another doorway. All around, the walls were hung with various western paraphernalia—some kind of polished animal horns, different kinds of antlers, a shelf of old cowboy boots, cracked leather ropes hanging in neat coils, all very satisfyingly cowboylike. Nothing in Cincinnati looked anything like this.

"We eat here all together," Stephen said. "Nora and Miguel, the cooks, go back and forth between the sections. The food's really good—Miguel makes great tortillas." He clumped up the right-hand staircase in the far corner. "This is the girls' side. Guys are on the other side."

At the top of the stairs, Stephen knocked at a partially open door. "Hey," he called. "I've got your roomie."

"Come on in," a gravelly voice called.

A rangy girl was sprawled on one of two metal beds, a journal open on the bed in front of her, a pen in her hand. "Hi," she said. "I'm Dana. Do you care which bed? I just took this one because it's closer to the door. I have to get up at like four in the morning to round up the herd."

"No, either's fine." I took my duffel from Stephen and placed it on the bed, then propped my guitar case by the door. It all sounded so western—wranglers and rounding up herds. Would that be horses or cows? Horses, I decided. I remembered that the ranch only kept a few cows to teach roping and cutting to the guests.

"Okay, well, Rick's expecting me over at the far pasture," Stephen said. "We're going to get the guests' horses cleaned up for tomorrow—they're riding for the first time." He rolled his eyes and I giggled. At the door, he turned. "By the way, staff meeting tonight after dinner. Jack wants to give everyone the rundown, work assignments, tell them about the rules."

"See you then?" I tried to keep my voice casual.

He looked right in my eyes and I froze momentarily. Then he nodded. "Definitely."

As his footsteps disappeared down the stairs, Dana raised her eyebrows. "I see you and Stephen are already friends."

"Oh . . . well . . ." I fumbled around, my face hot. "Anyway . . ." I cleared my throat and hoisted my duffel on to the bed.

"So, where're you from?" Dana asked as Stephen's footsteps faded down the stairs. She sat up and brushed her caramel-streaked blond hair from her face. "Is this your first time on a ranch? I'm guessing yes." She pointed to my sneakers.

I nodded, relieved at the change of subject. "Yeah, is it that obvious? I'm from Cincinnati. It's a long way from here. I guess you can tell."

Dana laughed and bounced up from her mattress. "It's okay, I've got you covered." She tugged with difficulty at a closet door, then rummaged around on the floor. "I only got here yesterday, and my stuff's already totally disorganized." She surfaced from the closet with a pair of battered cowboy boots in her hand and a dust ball hanging from her hair. "Here, are you an eight?"

"Seven and a half." I took the boots and looked at them with satisfaction. They were coated with a layer of seasons-old muck and dust and the heels were worn down. Very authentic cowboy. "You don't need these?"

"Nah." Dana motioned to the brown boots lying on the floor by her bed. "I've got these for this summer. I wore those last year. Unless you brought your own with you . . . ?"

"No, just some hiking boots." I pulled on Dana's boots and stood up. They felt odd on my feet, the heels unexpectedly high, but as I stamped around the room experimentally, I felt like I already had the proper western swagger in my step. I turned and, with a sudden warm impulse, hugged Dana quickly. "Thanks."

She squeezed back, seeming surprised but pleased. "No

problem." I looked in a spotted full-length mirror hung on the back of the door. My long, dark hair was windblown and the circles around my blue eyes made them look even bigger than usual, but with the boots, I felt like I already belonged out here on the range.

Chapter ● Three

"**M**ind some company?"

The voice came from behind me as I wandered down the long driveway that night after dinner. The staff meeting was supposed to start any minute, but I couldn't resist the cool allure of the air and the sunset that flung ruby, rose, gold, and lavender across the sky in a lavish array.

I turned around. Stephen was walking up rapidly behind me, a little out of breath. He must have trotted from the main house when he saw me leaving. His face shone faintly with perspiration. He'd changed his shirt into a soft blue button-down, sleeves rolled up. The auburn hair at his temples and around his forehead was damp, as if he'd just washed his face.

"Of course not." I smiled at him, pushing away the faintest stab of annoyance at being interrupted.

Stephen fell in step beside me. "I found these by the side of the bunkhouse." He proffered a slightly wilted bouquet of daisies and black-eyed Susans.

"Aw, that's so sweet." I smiled at him and took the flowers, which were warm from being clutched in his hand. I looked around, but of course I'd have to carry them. I couldn't just lay them down by the side of the road.

"We shouldn't walk too far. Rick doesn't like anyone being late for meetings." Stephen stuffed his hands in his pockets.

"No, I wasn't going to." Quietly, I transferred the flowers to my other hand and wiped my free palm on my shorts. The stems were bleeding green juice.

A silence fell between us—a little awkward in a way we hadn't been earlier by the pasture. The only sound was our feet scuffling in the dirt. I heard Stephen swallow with a little click. He cleared his throat, then took his hand out of his pocket. It swung loosely by his side, and I became aware of my hand swinging too—near his. He was going to try to hold my hand; I could sense it. We walked a little further. My hand felt like a piece of meat hanging at the end of my arm. Never had I felt so aware of an ordinary part of my own body.

Then I felt him swipe at my fingers like he was trying to capture an elusive bug, and he caught my hand in his. I tried not to break my pace or look down. Nothing obvious like that. Instead I moistened my lips and stared straight ahead at the end of the driveway, where the gray ribbon of the asphalt was just visible. Stephen's hand was hot and a little sticky—like my four-year-old cousin's. I tried to change my grip, to combat the stickiness.

"Maybe we should turn around," he said, before I could. We did a sort of awkward about-face, still holding hands, as if we were a drill team. It must have looked absurd to anyone watching from the porch—which I sincerely hoped no one was.

Thankfully, the porch was empty when we arrived back. Stephen let my hand go and I resisted the urge to wipe it on my shorts. "Well . . . thanks for walking with me." I smiled at him and he beamed back.

"Here." He opened the door for me and I stepped into the crowded common room. The dusky silent space of the afternoon was transformed now, with the big wagon-wheel lights flicked on, shedding their warm glow over the rows of packed heads. I found a seat beside Dana, stretched my booted feet out in front of me, and admired the effect. I hoped I looked like I'd been born wearing boots, with that slight cowboy swagger. "Who are all these people?" I whispered to Stephen, who sat on her other side.

"Well, you already met Jack. And that's Sandra, his wife." He pointed to a woman with graying blond hair tied back in a long braid, shuffling a stack of papers at the front of the room. Her face was weathered and wrinkled as if she'd spent many years in the sun and wind.

"Nora and Miguel, the cooks. They're married, too." The dark-haired couple stood in the kitchen doorway, their arms folded over their stained white aprons.

"Those sandwiches were amazing at dinner." My mouth was still burning from the peppers. "What did Miguel call them?"

"Tortas. And then there's the wranglers—Todd, Jeremy, and Chris," Stephen went on.

I eyed the three dusty guys slouched on a bench near the door, holding sweat-creased hats in their hands. Their plaid shirts and Wranglers looked as if they never took them off. "Those are the ones you work with?" I asked Dana.

My roommate grinned. "Yeah, those are my guys right there. Aren't I lucky? You can smell them a mile away."

Stephen continued. "And the rest are the maids, grounds guys, mowers. And my brother, Rick. He's the head trainer." A worshipful tone entered his voice as he indicated a larger, older mirror image of himself standing near the boys' staircase. He was different, though. He had a hardness around the mouth and eyes, a kind of inflexibility in his cross-armed stance.

"How much older is he than you?" I whispered.

"Eight years," Stephen said. Rick must have seen us looking at him, because he met my gaze without changing expression. I smiled back nervously, but the stony set of his face didn't change. "He's the most amazing rider—wait until you see him," Stephen went on. "Jack always says it's really Rick who runs this place."

I wondered if that was good.

At the front of the room, Jack cleared his throat. "People, listen up. Let's get started." He unfolded a pair of half-moon spectacles from his shirt pocket and put them on, then rocked back on his heels. "Welcome to Nickel River. We're going to work hard this summer, provide a pleasant time for our guests, and take excellent care of our stock."

The door banged open, cutting off Jack in midsentence. Everyone turned to look. Zach stood in the doorway, his black hair falling over his forehead, an apple in one hand. There was a little murmur and rustle through the crowd. My eyes widened. He had a lot of nerve showing up to the first staff meeting late.

Jack harrumphed and stared at Zach deliberately through his glasses.

"Sorry," Zach said, not sounding the least bit embarrassed. He sat down and crossed his ankle over his knee, cocked his arm over the chair back, and took a large, noisy bite out of the apple.

Jack had resumed talking at the front of the room. "I'd appreciate it if you all would arrive on time for all meetings."

Dana snickered. Zach looked around and spotted us. He winked and gave us a little sideways grin. Involuntarily, a giggle rose up in my throat, which I tried to squash. I looked away and tried to focus on the front of the room. Sandra was talking now.

"The comfort of our guests is our number one concern," she was saying in a soft voice. "We expect all of the summer help to look neat and presentable and be ready to help any guest at any time. You will be on time to meals, and under no circumstances are you to ride or take the horses anywhere without permission from myself, Jack, or Rick. In addition—" She held up a cell phone. "You might as well say good-bye to these for the summer. We barely get reception."

I slid my phone from my fleece pocket and glanced down at it quickly. Sandra was right. Zero bars.

"There is no Wi-Fi either," Sandra went on. "We have a dial-up connection in the main office. Any personal e-mails received for the staff will be printed out and distributed."

A few guffaws went up around the room. I sighed.

"It's not too bad," Stephen murmured next to me. His breath tickled my ear deliciously. "You get used to it."

Sandra handed out a daily schedule; then Rick stepped to the front of the room. "Listen up now. I've got your work assignments." He had a clipped way of speaking, as if he were biting off the end of each word. "Wranglers will be out every day with the herd, getting the guests mounted, making sure they don't kill themselves, driving the wagon, leading the trail rides. Summer hands will be doing horse care—mucking stalls, grooming, tacking up, filling the water tanks."

"I guess that's me," I whispered to Stephen.

"And me," he said. "Rick said we're short in our section, so I'm supposed to fill in."

My heart gave a little leap. "That's nice." I tried not to betray the cartwheels happening in my stomach. Visions of sunset watching on the pasture fence and trail rides up into the foothills swam in front of my eyes. Stephen was riding a black horse; I was on a white one. We rode side by side, and Stephen reached out and took my hand as the wind blew through our hair. . . .

"And Zach," Stephen went on.

The horses crumbled into dust.

"We're supposed to work together."

I resisted the urge to groan aloud.

The meeting concluded, and everyone rose from their seats. Jack, Sandra, and Rick strolled toward what must be their own residence, a large cabin set away from the other buildings. Nora and Miguel disappeared back into the kitchen.

"Come on." Dana grabbed my arm, her eyes sparkling. "We can't go to bed yet! We're going to have a fire out back. We have to celebrate our first night here."

I followed her out into the vast, black mountain night. The air was crisp and cool, carrying the scent of pine. I zipped my fleece up to my neck, glad I'd thought to bring it even though it was June. The grass rustled in the darkness, and the mountains were black shapes in the far distance.

A few people were already gathered around a metal ring set far back from the bunkhouse.

"Everyone pick up some kindling." Jeremy waved his arms in our direction. I scavenged along the ground as I walked. A big shrub to my right had some dead branches under it. I diverted over to it. "Going this way!" I called to Dana, who was headed to the left.

I stooped to pick up a good-sized branch with some kind of pine needles on it. The wood twisted in my hands and I felt the jab of a splinter sliding under my fingernail.

"Ow!" I dropped all my wood and squeezed my index finger in my other fingers briefly, then stuck the finger in my mouth.

"What's wrong?" a voice asked from the darkness.

I caught my breath and whirled around. Zach was standing behind me, some long sticks clutched in one hand.

"Nothing. Splinter."

He put his hand out and bent his head close. "I can't see it." He slid his phone from his pocket and by its ghostly light examined the dark shard caught just under the quick of my nail. I waited, trying not to be affected by the feel of his warm fingers around mine and his breath on my palm.

"There's a first aid kit in the house, isn't there? I'm sure it has tweezers." I started to withdraw my fingers, but he held on.

"No, look, I can get it out for you."

"How?"

Before I could move, he raised my finger to his mouth. At the touch of his lips, electricity shot straight through me. I inhaled sharply. He must have known the effect his touch had on me, because a little smile quirked the corners of his mouth. He grasped the tiny end of the splinter with his teeth and gave a quick tug.

"Here you go." He released my hand and removed the wood from the tip of his tongue.

I patted my hair, more to give my hands a task than for any other reason. "Thanks," I managed.

"No problem."

My heart had finally slowed to a normal rhythm by the time I settled on the rough, dry grass back at the campfire ring. Dana sat cross-legged beside me, and on the opposite side Zach slouched against a log. Jeremy put a handful of twigs in the fire pit and struck a match.

The twigs flared up, and the newspaper at the bottom curled into a glowing ball. Jeremy fed thin sticks into the fire one by one, until finally he propped three big split logs over the fire. Pine pitch popped, sending little flares of sparks into the night.

I leaned back against a rock, snuggling my hands in my pockets and crossing my legs. The fire toasted my face, while the cool air pressed at my back. The rough grass scratched the underside of my jeans. "So he said he was going to take this colt out, and he got this saddle and put it on backwards . . . ," Dana was saying to the girl on her other side. Someone handed me a bag of marshmallows. I took two and broke off a long stick from the pile by the fire.

One of the logs cracked and fell into the coals, shooting up sparks. I threaded my marshmallows on the stick and held them just above the flames. I watched them puff up, slightly hypnotized by the dancing fire.

"Chloe, where's your guitar?" Dana said. "Play for us!"

"Oh God, I'm not good. I know like two songs," I said.

"Go get it—we'll pass it around."

I rose from the circle and tramped through the house and upstairs, returning a minute later with my Gibson. I opened the case and tuned the guitar up. "Okay, here's my one song." I fumbled through "If I Had a Hammer," which my guitar teacher had taught me right before I left. Everyone clapped when I was through.

"Here, I'll play something," Stephen volunteered, and I gratefully passed the instrument over to him.

He arranged himself cross-legged and strummed a few chords. The sound was small in the vast night, but he looked very cute with a guitar in his hands.

"Michael, row your boat ashore, Hallelujah . . . ," Stephen sang in a reedy tenor.

I winced involuntarily. The song invariably reminded me of third-grade music class. And he was slightly off-key. I tried not to notice as I slid the charred skin off my marshmallows and stuck it in my mouth, then started toasting the insides again.

Zach caught my eye. Why was he staring at me? Because I let him get that splinter out?

He leaned over sideways, craning across the person in between us. "You have marshmallow on your face," he whispered.

I sat up and swiped furiously. He was laughing, of course. I slid back against my rock again, scrubbing at the sticky streak on my upper lip.

Stephen warbled through the final chords of "Michael, Row

Your Boat Ashore" with a few people gamely singing along. "Thanks, Stephen," Dana called out. "I felt like I was back at Camp Kern for a minute."

Then Zach leaned over and took the guitar out of Stephen's hands. "Here, man, take a break," he said. Stephen looked at him like he was going to protest, then shrugged.

"Knock yourself out."

I narrowed my eyes. But then Zach strummed a few opening chords, and the sound floated over, full and rich. "A little John Denver," he said to no one in particular, then sang in a clear baritone, *"He was born in the summer of his twenty-seventh year . . ."*

I sat up a little straighter, my burning marshmallows forgotten at the end my stick. Zach noticed and gave me a little sideways smile, as if he knew exactly what I was thinking. *"Coming home to a place he'd never been before,"* he sang.

I leaned back against my rock and tilted my head up to the diamonds-and-dust mess of stars filling the black night sky, more than I'd ever seen in my whole life. The music flowed over and around me, filling me up, smoothing my thoughts out.

The song ended and there was a little silence. "How about 'Country Roads'?" Chris, the ponytailed wrangler, called out. "Do you know that one?"

"Sure," Zach said after a long pause. *"I hear her voice; in the morning hours she calls me. The radio reminds me of my home far away,"* he began. He stopped. "Hang on." He cleared his throat. *"Country roads, take me home, to the place I belong, West Virginia, mountain mama, take me home, country roads . . . ,*" he sang. But his voice thickened and his fingers fumbled the chords. He stopped abruptly and jumped to his feet, handing the guitar to Stephen as everyone watched, surprised. "Sorry," he mumbled, not looking at anyone, and then rushed out of the circle, stumbling on a branch and disappearing into the darkness.

Dana and I looked at each other, eyebrows raised. There was something going on there.

Chapter ● Four

I balanced a boot on the bottom rail of the fence and pushed the hose over the edge of the huge galvanized water trough that sat just inside the gate. The clear, cold water gushed into the trough, which I'd just spent the last hour emptying out, scrubbing, rinsing, and now refilling. "Come on, guys, come and get it," I called across the grass to the grazing horses.

A few of them lifted their heads and pricked their ears at the sound of my voice. They'd already learned who brought treats and who didn't. Al and Diamond trotted across the grass toward me, probably hoping I was offering corn as well as water. I admired their beautiful stride as they broke into a canter, their heads high, Al graceful, Diamond a little stiff. I would never get tired of looking at them.

"Hey, boys," I said as they came up. I stroked their broad cheeks as they thrust their velvety noses into my hands, snuffling their moist, hot breath; then I held out the apple I'd saved from my lunch.

"Not the whole apple for you, Al," I told the bay as he tried to snatch it. I held on firmly and let him bite off half, then showed the other half to Diamond, holding the greedy Al away with my shoulder. "Stop. Don't be so piggy. Let Diamond have his." The old white horse sniffed my hand, then slowly crunched the sweet fruit, the juice dripping from his chin whiskers. He'd been one of the first horses on the ranch, Jack had told me, and for years he'd pulled the chuck wagon whenever they took the guests into the hills for a picnic. Then he was the pony-ride horse and patiently ferried hundreds of terrified and excited little children on his back, never once spooking or startling. He never even stepped on any of their feet. Now he was twenty years old, but Jack had let him retire out to pasture, which I thought was only fair, considering how hard Diamond had worked all those years.

I watched the horses relish their snack, then thrust their noses into the clear, cold water and drink it up eagerly. The trough was brimming full now. I shut off the hose and coiled it up on the spigot outside the fence.

Walking slowly back toward the stable, I examined two blisters on my palm and the blackened fingernail on my other hand, the result of an interview with Mickey's back hoof. I'd learned the hard way never to put tools down on the floor of the stall when I was grooming.

A couple of days had passed since my arrival, and the boots Dana had given me felt like mine. I'd picked hooves, toted saddles, and gone on one very windy expedition to catch horses in the far reaches of the pasture. I'd gotten the crazy little Taylor girls down from the roof of the stable, where they'd climbed and then gotten stuck. I'd brought a wet washcloth and a cup of tea for Mrs. Coleman, the young widow, after finding her sobbing one cloudy day, head down on the fence.

Ahead I spotted Stephen waving at me from the broad circle driveway in front of the stable. I hurried up to him, my heart beating a little faster. "Are you waiting for me?"

"Good morning, Blue Eyes." He flashed me a heart-melting smile. His hair was damp from the shower, and a charming trace of shaving cream was left on one cheek.

I reached over and wiped it off. "Good morning."

"Thanks." He ran his hand over his cheeks and neck. "The mirror was all fogged up. Hey, guess what just came in?"

"Oh, what? A surprise?"

"Yes. . . ."

"What? Tell me!" I clapped my hand together.

"No, guess." He grinned down at me, clearly enjoying the game.

I sighed in mock impatience. "A whole lot of Barbie dolls."

"I didn't know you were into Barbie dolls," he teased.

I laughed. "I'm not! I'm just guessing. . . . Okay, um, fifty pounds of Tootsie Pops."

"No . . ."

"Puppies."

He shook his head, grinning.

"Kittens."

"Time's up! Close your eyes and give me your hand."

You don't need to ask twice. I squeezed my eyes shut and felt his warm, strong fingers wrap around mine. I wondered if I'd be able to make it to wherever he was taking me with my knees in their present state of jelly-ness.

He led me over the stony path and through what I knew was the entrance to the barn, with its sweet, dusty smell of hay. We stopped. "Okay, open your eyes."

Three horses stood in the stalls opposite the door, hanging their heads over the half doors. One was a brown-and-white paint, one was black, and one was a buckskin, with tawny gray-brown fur and a black mane and tail. "Aw!" I breathed.

"We've got some newbies. Jack just bought them at auction." Stephen collected three halters from the bin by the door and hung one on the hook by each stall.

"Hi, babies!" I held my hand out to the black, then patted his neck firmly. "What are we doing with these guys?"

"Jack wants me to work with these new guys to get them ready to take on the overnight pack trip. They're all good camp horses, so it shouldn't take much to get them ready." He patted the black one on the shoulder. "And you're supposed to help me," Stephen went on. "So we get to work together." He grinned at me.

"Oh. Okay." My calm voice belied the handsprings going on inside me. I smiled at him and took a step closer. "It'll be fun."

I'd heard about this pack trip. It was the highlight of the summer, for the staff and the guests—a day's ride up into the mountains, across streams, on narrow trails, to camp under the stars. The whole section went, and the guests were already talking about it.

"That's what I was thinking." Stephen's eyes met mine.

"You get those horses in?" A loud voice from the doorway interrupted. Stephen's face tensed as Rick strode in.

"I got them off the trailer, no problems. The black didn't want to go in his stall, but I gave him some sweet feed and got him in that way." His voice was slightly too loud, slightly too eager. I shifted uncomfortably. I knew Stephen worshipped his brother, but Rick was kind of scary. He always seemed to be teetering on the edge of some kind of anger precipice.

Rick didn't reply. He looked the horses over carefully, running his hands over their heads and flanks, down to their legs, first the black, then the paint. When he got to the buckskin, the horse backed away and raised his head, trying to avoid the trainer's hands. "Come here," Rick muttered. He raised his hand to grab the horse's halter, and the buckskin trembled, his eyes rolling.

"Easy, boy," he murmured to the horse as he took hold of his head. Sweat streaked the animal's fur, as Rick continued his inspection.

"Jack's a damn fool," the trainer grunted, straightening up.

"How come?" I gathered my courage enough to ask.

Rick shot me a glance, as if he'd forgotten I was there. "Look there," he said, nodding toward the buckskin's head.

I stepped closer and stifled a gasp. The horse's forehead and cheeks and the sides of his neck and back were striped with scars—long, broad stripes of missing fur. "What happened?" I breathed, though I thought I knew.

"It looks like he's been beaten," Stephen said.

"He was heading for the meat factory, and Jack bid on him at the last minute." Rick took a toothpick from his breast pocket and stuck it in the corner of his mouth. "Pretty clear now why no one else wanted him."

"Oh, poor baby." I raised my hand to pat the horse, and he shied away again.

"Head shy," Rick said. "Watch yourself or you'll be missing a couple fingers. This horse can't go on the pack trip. I don't even know why Jack bought him. He needs to go straight back where he came from." He turned on his heel abruptly. "Tie that buckskin's head. He's going to bite anyone who comes near him." He clomped out into the bright sunshine.

Stephen sprang forward and fastened the horse's halter to a ring in the wall with a lead line. The horse's head drooped.

"What's going to happen to him?" I rested my chin on the top of the stall door. The horse craned his head to look at us. He looked so sad, tied up in the dark depths of the stall. "Does he really have to be tied?" I slid back the bolt and stepped into the stall. "There, boy," I crooned, stroking his shoulder and neck. He dropped his head a little further and I ran my hand up his neck. Gently, I patted his broad, flat cheek. He didn't jerk away this time. Instead he leaned up against me and pushed his heavy head against my arm.

"What's going to happen to you?" I whispered to him again. He heaved a great sigh and half closed his eyes.

"You like that horse, do you?"

I realized there was another figure in the barn aisle now, instead of one. I eased back out of the stall to see Jack standing beside Stephen.

Jack hooked his thumbs in his belt loops. "Glad you like this gelding, but he's just here for a couple weeks, Chloe. I only brought him with the others because Sandra couldn't stand to see him up there on the auction block." He smiled a little ruefully. "Forty years on the ranch and she still has a soft spot for the charity cases."

"But what then?" I couldn't keep the anxiety from my voice. "Where will he go after a couple weeks?"

Jack looked at me for a long moment. "I'm going to sell him again at the auction mart." He spoke gently. "He might get a home or he might go for meat."

"Meat!" Horror shot through me. Those big soft eyes and that gentle face going for meat! "No! You can't do that." The words were out of me before I remembered who I was talking to.

But Jack didn't take offense. He sighed. "I wish I didn't have to. But that's the way of horses. They're too expensive to keep if they're not earning it." He dropped a big, hard hand on my shoulder and squeezed. "He'll get a bit of a vacation here first, anyway."

Stephen and I looked at each other when Jack left. We were each hoping the other would speak first. "We should just turn him out," Stephen finally said. "Let him eat grass for two weeks. It might be the last time he gets to."

"Stephen, they can't send him back!" I cried, pain twisting my heart all of a sudden. "They can't! We have to keep him here."

"Jack won't. You heard him. He's really strict about all the animals here earning their keep. Old Diamond's the only one in retirement."

I pressed the back of my hand to my mouth. "I can't stand to think of him being . . . *eaten*." Even saying the word sounded grotesque.

"Hey, don't look so upset." Stephen took my hand, and my stomach fluttered in spite of my anguish. "Look, let's just make sure he has the best two weeks of his life."

"We can give him extra grain." I managed a smile.

"And let him stay out all night under the stars." Stephen took my other hand. The conversation wasn't just about the horse, I realized at the back of my mind.

His fingers were warm on mine. I took a tiny step closer to him. "And—"

"Hey, kids."

Zach tromped in all of a sudden, and I jumped, my foot hitting a metal bucket with a clang. "Oh, hi!" I tried to look casual, but his amused eyes told me he knew exactly what I was flustered about. "What are you doing here?"

"I work here, actually." He held out his hand. "Zach. Nice to meet you. I'm a summer worker—"

"Ha-ha." I swatted his hand away.

He grinned and dropped down on an overturned mud bucket. "To answer your question, I was told to come over here and groom the new horses. Is that okay with you, or did you have another activity in mind?" He wagged his eyebrows suggestively at me.

"That's fine," Stephen broke in. "You should do what you were assigned." He frowned at Zach, who slung a mocking arm around Stephen's neck and put him in a headlock.

"Absolutely, bro. You give the orders; I follow them."

Somehow I didn't quite believe him.

Stephen broke free of his hold and straightened up, his hair standing up. "The grooming boxes are in the tack room." He smoothed his hair down—a little fussily, I thought, then immediately chided myself. I sat down on a mud bucket.

"Hey, guys," Zach greeted the horses. "How was the ride over? Did you get to stop for food? Go through the drive-thru? Order grain burgers?" He rubbed the black under his forelock, then noticed the buckskin. "How come this one's tied?"

"Head shy," Stephen said, with his back to Zach. He didn't turn around.

"You should untie him." Zach sounded perfectly assured.

"What did you say?" Stephen slowly faced him, his voice incredulous.

"I said you should untie that horse's head," Zach said smoothly. "Tying up's the worst for a head-shy horse."

"How the hell do you know that?" Stephen said. "My brother told me to tie him up. Don't you think he would know, since he's the *trainer* here?"

Zach shrugged, apparently unruffled. "Yeah, you'd think so." He let that comment dangle in the air between the three of us.

Stephen was starting to get red in the face and puff. "Look, Zach," I put in, "Rick said to tie him up. We have to listen to what he says." A note clanged in the back of my mind, though, as I was speaking. We never tied our horses up in the stall at my stable. Still, Rick must know what he was talking about—he was in charge for a reason, after all.

But Zach got up, strolled over to the buckskin, and unlatched the door. The horse rolled his eyes and laid his ears back warningly, but Zach reached in, quick as an oiled snake, and pulled down hard on the safety-release catch of the lead line.

"Hey!" Stephen raised his voice. "Put that back! That horse bites, in case you didn't notice." A vein was throbbing in his neck.

Zach tossed the lead line, and Stephen caught it automatically. "Steve. If the horse is head shy, he's going to feel even more freaked out being tied up *by his head*. Then he'll never trust you." He spoke slowly, as if addressing someone of limited intelligence.

"If he *bites* someone, he'll be back to the glue factory!" Stephen shouted back, finally losing it. They were facing each other now, practically nose to nose.

Then Zach turned away abruptly. "No one's giving this horse a chance," he muttered. He strode over to the dusty window and gazed out, his hands jammed in his pockets. "He at least should have a chance."

His words sparked in my mind. "What did you say?" I asked slowly.

Zach's dark brow was knitted. "He should have a chance to at least try for a place here; that's what I said."

I jumped up from my mud bucket. "Do you think they'd give him an audition? If we worked with him, maybe?"

Stephen shook his head. "No. That's not the way Rick and Jack do it. It's okay. You guys haven't been around here long enough to know."

Zach caught my gaze and held it. Then the spark in me burst into flame. "Stephen!" I burst out. "It's like you and Rick. You said he won't give you a chance to try for assistant trainer—and this horse needs a chance too." I was pacing now, the words tumbling from me. "What if—what if this was your big break? What if we asked if we could train him up? And then Rick would see that you really do know a bunch? And he'd promote you and the horse could be saved!"

"Could work," Zach said from the window.

Stephen shook his head. "Chloe, I don't think they'd go for

it. They just don't do that around here. Rick makes up his mind and that's that."

"But why not just try?" I persisted. "You never know until you ask. We'll all go—the three of us."

"I'm for it," Zach said.

"Ah . . . I don't know. I need to think about it." Stephen strode out of the stable. Zach and I looked at each other, and then I hurried after him.

He was leaning on the pasture fence, his arms resting on the top rail, gazing out at the vast, waving grassland spread before us. Softly I came up next to him and leaned over the rail. I was silent and watched Diamond scratching his leg with his head. He switched his tail against the flies, and the breeze carried over the sweet-musty horse scent. To the west the mountains sat, calm, cool, blue-gray, and silent. Just gazing at them was restful. The grasses were rippling like water in the thin mountain air. Al was noisily slurping at the water tank, and somewhere very near my feet a cricket was trilling. I shifted slightly and the trilling stopped. I held very still. The trilling started again. A melody started in my head, combined with the cricket and the whistle of the wind—

"That guy can be kind of a jerk, don't you think?"

The words jarred me out of my reverie, and I glanced at Stephen. He was still staring ahead, hands clasped.

"Well . . ." I searched around for the right words. "I think we're all just trying to help the buckskin out, right?"

"He gets under my skin. I mean, how come he thinks he can

just barge in and take over like that?" I could see the muscles in Stephen's jaw clenched tight.

I cleared my throat. "Hey, um . . ." I cast around for some other, happier topic. "Which is your favorite horse?" I indicated the herd in front of us.

"Oh, I don't know." He furrowed his brow, thinking, and traced his thumb back and forth across the wooden rail. "Probably Hans."

"Hans?" I laughed. The German name sounded incongruous in this land of Jims and Big Bills and Codys. "Which one is he?"

"That one." Stephen leaned over to point. "That little fat chestnut beside the sagebrush."

He was very near to me now, his shoulder touching mine, and I felt his breath just touch my cheek.

"Oh yeah, I see him." Though at that moment I cared about Hans the Horse about as much as I cared about the state of North Korean politics. "How come he's your favorite?" I pulled myself together enough to ask.

"He's kind of an oddball—he's a Haflinger, which is this Austrian breed. The Amish use them a lot. They usually pull buggies, but Jake brought this one out here a while ago because we didn't have any ponies for the kids. But he's so strong, he can carry a man too. He's just a good little guy—totally willing, never offers to bite."

His voice trailed off and he glanced at me, then looked down quickly. He ran his fingers back and forth rapidly along the fence. "We can do it."

50

"What?"

"You were right. About talking to Rick. I was just getting all bothered by Zach being the one suggesting it. It's actually a really good idea." He smiled at me. "Sorry I was being stupid."

I threw my arms around his neck and gave him a quick hug. "Thank you! When should we do it?"

"Morning's the best time—they're usually in the office right after breakfast. We can do it tomorrow."

I squealed. "We're going to make him the best horse on the whole ranch—and Rick will see how amazing you are, I know it."

"I hope so." Then he paused and cleared his throat. "Hey, um, do you remember when we were driving in and saw the Garden of the Gods? Well, I was thinking of going for a hike out there tomorrow. We have the afternoon off. You want to maybe come with me?" The tips of his ears were bright red.

"Oh! Yeah! Yeah." I controlled my voice with an effort. *He's asking me out! He's asking me out!*

"Cool." He cleared his throat, regaining his composure. "I know this great trail—it's not marked, so no one goes on it, but my brother showed me once."

"I love secrets." My jaws ached from the strain of controlling my grin. "Sounds fun." *Or like heaven on earth. Whichever.*

"Stephen!" Rick's bark came from the hay shelter near the barn.

Stephen jumped as if he'd been pricked with a pin. "I have

to go." He threw me a quick smile. "Meet you after breakfast tomorrow?"

"Sure. I'll tell Zach." I watched as he scurried toward his brother, who was standing in a sweat-stained T-shirt, his fists on his hips.

I turned back to the pasture and rubbed my hand up and down Hans's warm nose, already wrapped in daydreams of tomorrow.

Chapter ✺ Five

The sky was heavy with gray-bellied clouds when I met Stephen and Zach on the porch of the main house after breakfast the next morning, still chewing my last bite of tortilla-and-egg sandwich.

"You guys ready?" Zach asked, looking from me to Stephen.

Stephen shrugged. "I can't guess what he'll say."

"No one's saying you can, bro." Zach's voice already held an edge of irritation.

"All right, let's go in," I said, cutting them off. I swung open the screen door with more confidence than I felt.

Rick and Jack were sitting on either side of a battered metal desk heaped with papers, stirrup leathers, bits, and hay samples. In the corners of the stuffy little office, feed buckets were stacked five high, and the walls were hung with old and out-of-service bridles.

I half admired a silver mounted one as we crowded the doorway.

Jack looked at us over his glasses. "What is it, folks?"

We wedged ourselves into the cramped space. Rick pushed his chair back with a scrape. "You hands need to get to your work."

"We have a request for you first," Zach said. He sounded so calm and direct.

"We were wondering if you'd let us work with the buckskin horse," I said. "I know you said he's only here temporarily, but we were thinking that maybe if we trained him up some, he could be a good ranch horse—and he could stay." I stopped, my breath arrested in my throat.

"No." Rick didn't even bother to look at us. He opened a file folder on his lap and took out a schedule and handed it to Jack. "Get to work."

That was it. Dismissed. Impotent anger choked me. He wasn't even going to offer an explanation.

"That horse deserves a chance!" Stephen suddenly burst out. I could feel his arm trembling against mine. "No one's sending him away without at least giving him a chance."

Jack put down the schedule.

"What did you say?" Rick asked slowly. Dangerously.

Jack stood up and pulled three feed buckets from the corner. "Sit down, you three."

We sat.

"Now, tell me what's going on here." Jack spoke to all of us, but he was looking at Stephen.

"We feel like the buckskin could be a good horse, sir," Zach jumped in smoothly. "He has potential. Chloe, Stephen, and I can school him every day. If he's not doing good in a month or two, send him back to the auction then. That's our proposal."

"I can do this," Stephen broke in. He was talking to Rick. "Just wait. He'll be the best guest horse on the ranch."

"If you're looking to be assistant trainer because of this horse, there's no promises." Rick spit the words out like apple seeds.

I cringed. Stephen looked straight ahead, where there was a yellowing poster of shoeing procedures. Zach whistled a little between his teeth and leaned back against the wall, supremely unconcerned.

"It's up to you," Jack said to Rick. "Their daily work won't suffer much. I'm willing to give the old boy a chance if these three think they can train him up." He smiled at us.

"All right." Rick looked us over as if we were destined for the auction mart too. "Here's the deal. We're short horses for the pack trip. You get that buckskin ready in time. If he can do the trip, he can stay." He turned his back without waiting for a response.

The conference was over, and we hurriedly got off our buckets. "We'll see about assistant trainer," Rick called after Stephen as we were leaving. "We'll see how that horse does."

Back on the porch, I let out a big breath I hadn't realized I'd been holding. "We did it!" I clapped my hands together. Zach gave me a high five.

"You were awesome!" I hugged him, and he lifted me off my feet and twirled me around.

Stephen was standing quietly to one side, watching us. I felt a sudden flush of guilt, as if I'd been caught. I laid my hand on his arm. "Aren't you happy? This is your chance at assistant trainer. We'll show Rick how great the buckskin can really be." My voice was uncharacteristically bubbly.

"Yeah. Yeah. We will." Stephen smiled, finally.

Zach slapped Stephen's shoulder. "Come on, man. We're driving out to the west pasture to scrub water troughs."

"I'm supposed to turn out, so I'll let you guys know how it goes," I called over my shoulder as I hurried across the wind-whipped grass toward the stable.

I examined the chore chart pinned to the dusty bulletin board by the door. *Auction horses—halter, lead line, pasture,* it said. Perfect. That meant I was supposed to work on the ground with the new horses, getting halters on them, leading them around, making sure they had good ground manners—no biting the lead line, or trailing behind, or stopping to snatch grass. Then I would have to take them out to the pasture, make sure they knew how to go in and out of the gate, introduce them to the other horses. General getting-to-know-your-new-home activities. I could start working with the buckskin this morning.

I took down a lead line from the wall. "Hey, good morning, guys," I greeted the black and the paint, who were hanging over the half doors of their stalls, ears pricked, clearly waiting for visitors. I gave the black a scratch on the star on his broad forehead, and the paint poked his nose over. "You want your share too, don't you?" I rubbed his velvety nose, pricked with stiff whiskers.

The buckskin wasn't hanging his head over like his friends. Instead he was huddled at the back of his stall, as far from the front as he could get. I peeked over the door, and as soon as the buckskin saw me, he rolled his eyes and pressed himself against the back wall. My heart ached for him—he was so afraid of people, there was no doubt he'd been abused. I stood for a moment, thinking, then went down to the feed room and returned in a moment with a scoop of sweet grain in a bucket. No horse could resist this mixture of oats, wheat, and corn coated with a layer of sticky molasses. I gave the black and the paint each a handful in their feed buckets so they wouldn't feel left out, then shook what was left enticingly at the buckskin. "Here, boy," I crooned. He could hear the others crunching now. I dumped a handful into his feed bin. "Here, come get a snack, boy." Then I casually strolled down the broad aisle to the front doors, where the dust motes danced in a beam of sunlight.

Behind me I heard more crunching. I turned around. The buckskin was eating his treat, ignoring the questing noses and eager snuffles of his neighbors. I smiled to myself. The first hurdle crossed.

Slowly, casually, I strolled back to the stall, as if I were just stopping by. The paint saw me coming and gave an eager little whicker, hoping for more snacks, no doubt. This time the buckskin remained at the front of the stall. I gave them each another small handful. The buckskin needed no encouraging now that he saw I was going to give him treats and not yell at him or yank his head around.

This time I stayed in front of his stall as he crunched his grain. I chatted with him softly, just meaningless words, giving him a chance to get used to the sound of my voice. Meanwhile I took a currycomb and rubbed it up and down the paint's throat, which one of the horses at my old stable used to love. The paint loved it just as much and half closed his eyes, raising his head up very high and swaying back and forth, pressing against the currycomb. Then I casually moved on to the black, rubbing him softly behind the ears with my fingertips, like a horse massage. He liked that, so I began stroking his ears very softly with both hands. It relaxed him so much that he dropped his head lower and lower, his ears relaxing out to the sides until he looked like a donkey.

I knew the buckskin was watching us, so slowly yet firmly I reached over and patted him low down on the neck, far away from his head. "There, buddy." He didn't flinch, so I patted him a little higher up. Still okay.

I slid back the bolts on the stalls and slipped halters onto the black and the paint—no problems there—and led them out to the pasture, where they easily went through the gates.

Now for the buckskin. He was already relaxing and I didn't want to push him, but I also didn't want to face Rick and have to tell him that a whole day had gone by and I hadn't even gotten a halter on him.

Smoothly, with no sudden movements, I unlatched his stall, the halter over my arm. He eyed me, quivering slightly, but did not back away or flatten his ears. "Hey there, boy," I crooned. Before he had time to look at the halter too much, I draped the lead line over his neck and slid the halter up over his nose and behind his ears, then fastened the throat latch. There, I'd done it! We stood there, looking at each other, both of us equally surprised, I think. He was wearing his halter. The trick was not to make a big deal out of it or get into some kind of long buildup where he had time to think about it and get agitated.

Now came the next part: getting him out of the stall and into the pasture. I had no idea how he'd do on a lead line or what his experience had been with being led, but I tried not to let my tension communicate itself through my body. I'd learned at my old stable that horses are masters of body language. They can sense tension in your hands right through the reins or a lead rope.

So what I needed to communicate to the buckskin was that being led out to the pasture would be a pleasurable and unimportant event. You would never want him to think that this was a big deal to you in any way—that would equal tension in him, which, in a horse like this, could lead straight to explosions.

Trying to keep all this at the front of my mind, I smoothly slid back the bolt and, taking a firm grasp of the rope under his chin, with the rest looped neatly in my other hand, I led him from the stall. Not dragging, not allowing him to get ahead of me, but also not looking at him, I asked him to walk calmly beside me down the wide cement aisle toward the enticing blue-and-yellow square of the outdoors visible at the other end.

The moment we stepped out of the stall, I felt his body tense. He raised his head and sniffed the sweet fresh air. His hooves clopped a little faster behind me. I led him across the dusty, bare spot in front of the stable and across to the pasture gate. We paused at the water trough, where someone had left the hose still running. The buckskin froze, jerking his head up and snorting suddenly.

My hand tightened on the lead rope and I instinctively looked toward the trough, expecting to see a snake or a lizard near the edge. But there was only the clean galvanized steel and the clear water flowing from the hose. "What is it, boy?" I stepped closer to him, trying to calm him with the nearness of my body. The horse's eyes were wide, the whites visible. His nostrils flared, showing the edge of pink deep inside. His gaze was fixed on the trough.

"Is it the water?" I said softly. I tried to lead him toward the pasture gate. He would walk with me, but wouldn't allow his body near the trough, so he walked with his head turned as if the trough and he were opposing magnets. I led him through the gate and once more tried to lead him up to the trough. Was it the hose? The trough itself? Holding the lead rope with one hand, I quickly turned off the water at the spigot and shoved the hose away with one foot. Now the surface of the water was no longer burbling and bubbling.

The buckskin relaxed, as if someone had turned off a switch, and lowered his head to the trough. He sucked up big mouthfuls of water with long slurping noises. I unclipped the lead rope and stroked his mane absently as he drank. It was the hose, then—maybe the way it made the water look? It couldn't be the hose itself, I decided, as the buckskin finished drinking and raised his head. It was lying right by my feet, and he was paying no attention to it. If he were afraid of the hose, like he would be if someone had beaten him with one, he still wouldn't want to come near it. It must have been the way the hose made the surface of the water burble and bubble. Or the noise, perhaps.

The buckskin raised his head from the water and turned his neck, looking across the pasture at the horizon. The other horses were just visible as specks, grazing on the vast plain of grass. I stepped back, watching, entranced. The warm wind lifted the buckskin's rough black mane, twisting his forelock off his forehead. He raised his nose and let out a little whinny. The wind carried the sound to the other horses, and faintly an answering nicker came floating back. The horse trotted toward the sound, breaking into a long, easy canter. His feet beat the ground rhythmically, and it seemed impossible that he would ever stop. *He should be called Magic,* I thought as I closed and latched the gate. He looked like magic when he ran.

Chapter ✦ Six

Sweaty and dusty after the chores, I pushed open the screen door to the bunkhouse and hurried toward the kitchen for a drink of water. My mouth was so dry, it felt lined with flannel. The doorway to the kitchen was a brightly lit square in the dimness of the main room, and the sound of voices and clattering dishes issued from the opening. "Miguel," I called, leaning over the service counter, "can I come in and get—"

I stopped short, the words still in my mouth. Zach was standing at the long stainless-steel prep table, an apron around his neck, kneading a huge pile of dough. Nora stood beside him, wearing those plastic-bag gloves, scooping handfuls of the dough as Zach kneaded it, rolling it into discs.

"Nice apron." I grinned at Zach, recovering myself. "I thought you were scrubbing water troughs."

"I was, but Nora needed a volunteer for these tortillas. I was the natural choice, of course."

I raised my eyebrows. "Oh, of course." He had a dab of flour on his cheek and more in his hair. "Miguel, do you mind if I get a glass of water?"

Miguel nodded from his post at the eight-burner stove, where he was sautéing beef and onions together. The aroma made me want to go over there and stuff it all in my mouth with my hands.

I eyed Zach as I took a glass from the cupboard. His hair was tousled boyishly, and the apron contrasted with his tanned, muscled arms.

I wandered over and leaned on the counter as Nora handed Zach the rolling pin. "Here now, Zachary, enough of the lesson. You try it."

"You both just want to see me mess up." He took the pin, holding it like a club. "I'm outnumbered here."

I giggled but then stopped as he deftly rubbed flour on the rolling pin, then flattened a scoop of dough with his palm and rolled it flat with a few swift strokes. Nora raised her eyebrows. "Zach, you don't have too much to learn. Here I was, giving you a lesson for half an hour, and I can see you already know plenty." She laughed and pushed the bowl toward him. "You two finish this up. The delivery truck is here anyway." She walked toward the back, chuckling.

An apron flew through the air, hitting me in the face. "Hey!" I pulled it from my head.

"Stop slacking off, McKinley. I need an assistant." He tossed a ball of dough lightning quick, and I just managed to catch it.

"Are you playing with your food?" I threw it back and slipped the apron over my head, then stared at the pile of dough. "Okay, so what do I do with this?"

"Just knead it." Zach rolled out another tortilla.

I gave the dough a tentative punch with my fist. "Like this?"

"What, are you mad at it? Here." He pressed the heels of his hands into the dough and tromped them up and down.

I tried the tromping motion too, but apparently I wasn't doing it right, because Zach sighed and shook his head. "Dude, you need to put some muscle into it." He leaned over my shoulder and covered my hands with his. My pulse zoomed up at his closeness, but I tried not to stiffen up. His hands were much bigger than mine, the skin of his forearms darker. I could feel the muscles of his chest pressing against my upper back. And I could smell him too—a cedary scent, like some kind of soap.

His hands pressed down on mine, much harder than I had been pressing. "There, see? You have to really get into it." He took his hands away and looked toward the doorway, running the back of his hand over his forehead. I looked down at the dough, trying to calm my breathing.

Miguel switched on the vent fan, and the background noise helped me recover myself. I flopped the dough over and started dividing it into smaller balls. Zach began on another tortilla, his hands flying. "All right, so confess. How come you know how to do this?" I nodded at his deft movements.

He shrugged with one shoulder. "My mom had a little café in Charleston when I was like ten—just for a couple years." A rueful expression crossed his face. "We were between stepfathers."

"What was it like?" I rolled a wad of dough between my palms. "The café, I mean. Not being between stepfathers."

He dipped into the flour canister at his side. "It was actually outside of Charleston, on Johns Island. But it's super country out there."

"Like cows and corn and stuff?" I handed him a dough ball.

He laughed and shook his head. "Like little cabins from a hundred years ago, falling over, with huge vines growing all over them. And these trees—they're called live oak trees; they don't don't have them up here—with giant branches that make kind of a canopy over the road and the fields. It gets really, really hot and super humid and the bugs are just huge. And the neighbors used to burn their trash in the drainage ditches by the side of the road, so there'd be fire on both sides of your car when you drove past." He stopped to take a breath.

"Wow." I stared at him, my hands still. "You must miss it." I remembered the dough and began another pile of balls.

He nodded. "Yeah. I miss the food, too."

"Which? What was the best food in your café?"

"Probably the green beans. My mom would do them with

onion and bacon, and she'd simmer them all morning. Once, when I was little, I snuck in and ate the whole pot. She was so mad I thought she was going to throw me right out the door." He laughed, his face alight.

I laughed too. "You bad little boy. I once ate a whole bowl full of sugar."

"Are you kidding?" He added another tortilla to the growing stack at his elbow.

"I'm not! My mom was super strict about sugar, and I wasn't allowed to have *any*. So I snuck over to my friend Damien's house next door one day when I was supposed to be taking a nap and just ate huge fistfuls. I finished the whole bowl before they found me. Here. This is the last." I gave him the final few dough balls, then leaned my elbows on the table as he rolled them out. "I'm starving."

"Here." Zach held out an uncooked tortilla.

"Ew, no thanks." I wrinkled my nose.

"Dude, it's good." He bit off half. "Dan used—" He stopped suddenly, and a grimace passed over his face.

"Who's Dan?" I reached out and took the other half of the tortilla from his hand, stuffing it into my own mouth. He was right—it wasn't too bad. Like un-sweet cookie dough. "Who's—" I stopped. His mouth was drawn, and the light had gone out of his face.

"My brother." His voice was oddly muffled. He looked down fixedly at the stack of tortillas.

"Oh." I was about to ask him where his brother was, but before I could, Zach grabbed a baking sheet from under the counter.

"These can go in the oven." He started shoveling the tortillas onto it without meeting my eyes. "So, that was awesome this morning, with the horses."

I sensed he was trying to change the subject. "Yeah. It really was. Thanks for speaking up like that. Jack and Rick weren't even listening to Stephen or me." I studied his face. He didn't want to talk about his brother—that much was clear. Why, though? What was the secret?

"Well, it was stupid not to give him a chance. He can do it. He's a good horse. You can see it in his face." He opened the oven and a puff of heat hit us. Zach leaned away and slid in the baking sheet.

"You can. And he has such a pretty mane, too. I found some detangler this morning—I was going to comb it out. I could braid it too—I learned at my old barn."

"Whoa, Nellie. All the other horses will make fun of him." He grinned at me, the teasing light back in his face.

"He'll look cute." A timer dinged somewhere, and Nora hurried back in, with Miguel close behind.

"Where are the tortillas?" she asked, looking around.

Zach nodded toward the oven. "I couldn't stop Chloe once she got started. She was like a tortilla-making machine. Seriously, I couldn't hold her back. She had all those puppies rolled out in like five seconds."

"He's such a liar," I told Nora. "All I did was knead. He did the rest."

"Don't believe her! She should be on kitchen duty the rest of the summer—she's like a professional chef!"

"You're a nut job," I laughed, shoving him out of the kitchen in front of me. "You shouldn't be trusted."

He raised his eyebrows. "*That's* for sure." He leered at me, and I rolled my eyes as I headed for the stairs.

"How was the trail ride this morning?" I stood in front of the wavery, spotty mirror in our bedroom that afternoon. Dana was propped up on her bed, her wet hair wrapped in a towel, wearing sweatpants and a tank top and scribbling rapidly in her journal with a chewed-up Bic.

She groaned without looking up. "Those little girls are such brats!"

She meant the Taylors' kids—they'd proven themselves to be every bit as out of control as we'd previously thought.

Dana leaned over and put her journal in the drawer of her bedside table, then lay back again against the pillows. "I'm trying to get the dad mounted and he's being, you know, the way big men are, all stiff and scared but trying not to show it. Making dumb jokes, clutching the saddle horn. So I'm just trying to keep him upright on Mickey, when I look over and they've both gotten on Hans! Without helmets! Which, if Jack saw, he would proba-bly fire me and eat them for breakfast."

I nodded. Helmets weren't the most attractive headgear and certainly didn't fit my picture of myself galloping in a field of grass with my long hair flowing out behind me, but they were nonnegotiable. Jack had given us a massive lecture about liability. Apparently he could get sued for everything he owned if an accident happened to one of us staff or a guest on a horse and they weren't wearing a helmet.

"So poor Hans is trying to keep from freaking out, but I can see he's getting all trembly and sweaty, and in a minute he's probably going to dump them." Dana put her hand over her eyes as if to shut out the memory. "And I'm all by myself, you know, since they were supposed to get on one at a time, and now I'm freaking out, my heart is pounding, I'm thinking that this is it, Hans is going to throw those little girls into a tree and then Mickey will spook and dump the dad and they'll have go to the emergency room and then I'll be back in Boise, working at Wendy's for the rest of the summer." She stopped to take a breath.

"And? Come on, don't leave me in suspense here!" I said.

"Wait, it gets better. So the dad sees what's going on now—he didn't before because he was trying not to fall off—and he shouts at the girls to get off the horse. And Hans thinks he's shouting at *him*, so he starts trotting off, probably going back to his stall, and I swear to God, the bigger girl *jumps off Hans* like she's some kind of stuntman, and does a somersault in the dirt. By now I'm yelling, trying to catch Hans, the dad's gotten off Mickey somehow, he's yelling, the big girl's screaming, and Hans goes straight into the stable and I run after him. He's in his stall with the little girl still on his back."

"Oh my God," I said.

"So I grab the little girl off Hans, slip his bridle off, and go back out—Mickey's gotten the lid off one of the outside grain bins and is eating everyone else's lunch," Dana concluded.

"That's crazy! Were the girls okay?"

My roommate flopped back against the pillows, crossed her eyes, and let her tongue loll out the side of her mouth. "Yeah, they were fine."

I stood up and rummaged around in the top drawer of her dresser, then extracted a hairbrush. "Here, I'll French-braid your hair," I offered. "That'll be relaxing."

"Oh, yay, thanks!" She sat up and turned around on the bed, unwinding the towel from her head.

I knelt behind her and began pulling the brush through her wet blond locks. "Zach and Stephen and I came up with this plan to keep that one horse Jack brought from the auction mart."

"The one who'd been beaten?" Dana had her eyes closed. "I thought he was some kind of charity case."

"He was. I mean, he is." I updated her on the session with Jack and Rick. "We're allowed to try him out—the pack trip is going to be his big test." I tugged at a snarl.

"Ow! I'll help you. Just tell me when you want to try him on a trail."

"And . . ." I drew out the word. "I'm going to Garden of the

Gods with Stephen in an hour." My stomach gave a little flip of excitement just saying it. I'd almost forgotten about the date with all that had happened this morning.

"Aww, that's so cute," she said. "Is it a date?"

I frowned, and picked at a tangle. "I don't know. I think so. What do you think?"

"Hmm. Is anyone else going?"

"No. . . ." I set the brush aside and picked up a few locks of hair at the top of her head. "Well, he didn't say if there are. And he said he'd show me this secret trail."

"And he asked you specifically—like, 'will you go with me'?"

I twisted more hair into the braid, admiring the way the lighter strands looked against the darker ones. Blond hair always looked best in a French braid, so much better than brown. "Yeah, yesterday, when we were out by the stable." I braided the last section and wrapped a hair tie around it. "There, that looks really good."

Dana sat up and trailed her fingers along the intricate weaving on the back of her head. "You got it so tight—thank you! That's my favorite way." She went over to the mirror and looked at the back with a mirror compact. "Well, I'd say if he asked just you and he wants to show you his favorite secret trail, then that's a date. He totally likes you! Aren't you excited?" She turned around and grasped both my hands, pulling me up from the bed. "He likes you, he likes you, he likes you!" she sang, dancing me around the room.

I collapsed on my bed, giddy now from the dancing and from the heady thought that Stephen might actually like me. Then I jumped up. "I have to decide what to wear!" I flung open my closet and pulled out several options. Dana sat back down on the bed, as serious as an editor at a fashion show.

"Okay, option one." I pulled on a gray T-shirt that read WINTER JAM. "This is like the cool girlfriend who wears her boyfriend's clothes."

Dana nodded. "Check. Guys like that."

"But maybe a little boring?"

She considered. "Maybe."

I held up my hand. "No fear." I tugged the T-shirt over my head and shimmied into a black tank top. "Also sporty, but a little cuter. Also a little more girly."

"Hmm, I like that one. And it shows off your tan." She tapped her fingers on her front teeth. "Any others?"

I riffled through my clothes hangers as if shuffling cards. "Just a last one—I don't know about the long sleeves, though." I pulled out a thin western-style shirt with pearl snaps in a soft pink-and-blue plaid. "My mom bought it for me when I decided to come out here."

"Cute! Put it on," Dana said, then considered me as I snapped it up. "That fits great. And you have the whole cowgirl look going, which is adorable."

I stared at myself in the mirror. "But what about the long sleeves?"

"Here." She jumped off the bed. "Do them like this." She rolled them to my elbow, then undid one more snap down the front. "There. It looks cute. And you look like a real Colorado chick, which Stephen will love. His last girlfriend was a native, you know."

"*Last* girlfriend." I sank down on the bed and stared at her. It hadn't even occurred to me that of course he must have had others. "What was she like? How 'last' was she?" I parted my hair in the middle and started twisting one side into a braid.

Dana tilted her head. "Um, let's see—well, it was last summer and she was one of the maids. I think she was a year older than him. They were super gushy—like every second you saw them together, they'd be holding hands. He called her Button, seriously."

"No!" I snorted laughter. *"Button?"*

Dana nodded. "Oh yeah, it was nauseating. I think they were in touch all year until pretty recently. Maren. That was her name. She was really short, like five feet, and sort of cute—really blond, blue eyes."

I finished doing my second braid and put down my brush. My giddiness trickled away like air from an old balloon. "And they were gushy?"

Dana sat down beside me on the bed. "She was totally annoying. Everyone thought so."

"Except Stephen."

"Yeah." Her voice was reluctant. "And Rick, actually. I think they knew each other from school. He used to go down to the laundry room and flirt with her." She frowned. "Then Stephen and Rick had a big fight—over her, I guess. It was bad. They got into it during dinner one night, and Stephen actually shoved Rick over a bench. I thought Rick was going to tear Stephen's head off with his bare hands. Both Jack and Miguel had to hold him back."

"Seriously?" I stared at her. "I can't believe Stephen would hit Rick. He always seems kind of scared of him."

Dana shrugged. "Maybe he was mad his brother was flirting with Maren. It *was* pretty egregious of Rick. We were all kind of shocked he would be that obvious about it. Anyway, Stephen practically crawled on his knees in front of Rick the rest of the summer."

I could believe that. "What happened to Maren?"

"She left early. Some story about a place in an acting program opening up. But I think she wanted to leave after all that drama." Dana got up from the bed and picked up her toothbrush.

I stood up too, but more slowly. My mind was swimming with all she'd told me. I had the sense of a muddy, slow-moving river coursing beneath the peaceful pastures of the ranch. The water was murky and dark with memories.

Chapter ✺ Seven

I walked down the dusty little path that twisted among thick clumps of silver-white sagebrush. The ground under my feet was hard, baked, the dirt a rich rosy orange. Reddish dust powdered my hiking boots and the hem of my jeans. Towering red rock rose on either side of the path. Their faces were faintly rough, porous, like adobe—not like Ohio's shale. The corners of these giant rocks were rounded, holes and bridges carved out by thousands of years of wind. Some were twisted into weird shapes—little towers swirled like ice cream; round balls balanced on spires; platforms of rock extended out from the sheer sides. Every huge rock was studded with dozens of small holes, and now and then we passed a couple of rock climbers, clinging to the walls like giant, brightly colored spiders.

The air down on the trail was absolutely still, held in by the sun-warmed rocks, and scented with the sharp fragrance of sage. I stopped to inspect a little orange-and-purple flower that grew close to the ground. It reminded me of a little flame held between stiff green leaves. "Indian paintbrush," Stephen said, stopping beside me. "And those are roses." He pointed to a brambly bush with simple, white flowers.

"Really?" I looked more closely at the flowers. "They don't look like roses."

"They're wild, so they look different. Smell them, you'll see."

I sensed his eyes on me as I bent down. The scent was strong and sweet in the warm, still air. "Mmm. You're right." I straightened up and caught him staring at me. I swallowed and smiled back, and suddenly the air between us was electric, as if energy had passed back and forth.

"How do you know about flowers?" I asked as we started walking again. I was behind him now, and looking at his back made it easier to talk.

"I like stuff like that," he said over his shoulder. "I'm the nerd reading wildflower guides for fun."

I remembered I hadn't told him about my discovery about Magic earlier. "Hey, I had a revelation about the buckskin earlier." I recounted the trough incident. "So, my theory is that he's afraid of running water." I looked at Stephen sideways to gauge his reaction. "What do you think? Like maybe someone tried to force him to get near water, maybe the same person who beat him?"

Stephen nodded, thinking. "Yeah, that definitely seems

possible. We'll have to test it out some more." He was quiet, walking beside me on the path, his tanned hands wedged into the shoulder straps of his backpack.

I cast him a glance. "What are you thinking about?" I winced a little as the words came out of my mouth. Ryan Davis had once told me that guys hated that question.

Stephen raised a finger to his mouth and gnawed at a nail. "Not much. Did you think Rick mean what he said this morning?" His forehead was furrowed. "About assistant trainer, I mean." A slight note of desperation had crept into his voice. I looked at him more closely. He continued to gnaw his fingernail. His other nails were bitten to the quick.

"I don't really know him that well," I said carefully. I felt like I had stepped unknowingly off the boardwalk in a bog. There might be quicksand nearby, but I didn't know where it was.

"This is it. Rick's finally giving me a chance." Stephen continued to bite his fingers.

I stopped on the path and gently pulled his hand from his mouth. Blood rimmed the top of his index fingernail. We both looked down at it; then our eyes met. He shifted his grasp so that he was holding my hand. I inhaled. He gazed at my face an instant longer, then released my hand.

We started walking again. The path inclined slightly now. The giant red rocks were behind us, giving way to arid scrub. Stephen's footsteps scrunched on the dusty gravelly path. After a minute, he spoke. "It's just my brother. It's like my whole life, I've never been good enough for him. I'm always the one trying; he's always the one deciding. Even when we were younger, my dad would put him in charge of the chores, and if I didn't do them right, he'd whip Rick with a yardstick."

I winced. "Seriously?" Stephen's dad sounded like the dad in *The Red Pony*, the John Steinbeck novel we'd read last year in English. In other words, totally scary.

Stephen nodded. "That's just how it is out where we are." He shrugged. "Rick won't admit that I'm not ten anymore, though." His voice rose in frustration. "I'm never good enough for him— just like when we were little."

We were halfway up the incline, and I was definitely puffing now. I sank down on a large flat rock to one side of the path and dug my water bottle from my backpack. "Rick kind of scares me," I admitted, taking a big gulp of water to clear my dust-parched throat.

Stephen remained standing on the path, hands looped under his backpack straps again, gazing off toward the top of the hill. "He's not a bad guy. He just likes to see us do right, that's all. He doesn't mean to come off so harsh."

I stood up and shoved my water bottle back into my pack. We started up the incline again.

"Vulture." Stephen pointed above us.

I squinted up. "How can you tell? I thought it was a hawk."

He gazed at it, his head tipped back and his curling auburn hair brushing the collar of his T-shirt. "The wings. Vultures are darker, and their wings have these separate feathers that curl up at the end a little. Vultures also tip back and forth in the air. Hawks hold perfectly still."

I stared at the big black bird soaring in the azure sky. "I can see the ends of the wings, just like you said."

He didn't respond, and I looked over and caught him watching me.

"What is it?" I put my hand to my hair, suddenly self-conscious.

He paused. "Your eyes are so blue." Then he flushed and started walking again so quickly he stumbled over a rock.

I was glad he was in front of me so he wouldn't see the smile I couldn't keep off my face.

Stephen stopped. "There it is!"

I looked around. We were standing in the middle of the path surrounded by rocks and trees, and a small blue lizard perched on a rock by my foot. "What?"

"The secret trail I was telling you about. We have to crawl through here." Stephen pushed aside the boughs of a small pine tree, and bending down, I saw a tunnel in the rock face behind it. It looked deep and very dark.

"Seriously?" My voice sounded a little squeaky. "Go through there?"

"Yeah, go ahead." Stephen held the branches to one side for me. "You'll have to crawl. The trail's on the other side. There's an amazing overlook at the top."

I did *not* want to look like a prissy girl in front of Stephen, so I crouched down and started wiggling through. I wondered how big my bottom looked from his angle. "Did I mention that I panic in small spaces?" I called out the opening.

"You're doing fine," he called back in. "Keep going."

The tunnel was cool and the rock slightly damp. It was only about fifteen feet long but a tight enough fit that I felt a wave of claustrophobia envelop me. I made myself take two deep breaths and thought of the time I'd gotten stuck in a similar tunnel at the playground when I was babysitting. A queue of annoyed preschoolers and their mothers had watched for an embarrassingly long time as I tried to pry myself out. I banished the thought of Stephen having to push me through the tunnel and heaved myself out the other end, flopping onto the dirt and gasping like a beached fish.

I climbed to my feet quickly and dusted off my front while Stephen nimbly wiggled through, already scanning the rise of a slope just ahead of us. "Here we go!" He pointed to a small path weaving through the brushy ground, then grabbed my hand, and together we climbed, panting, up the last rise of the mountain.

Halfway up I stopped, resting my hands on my knees, my lungs straining in the unaccustomed altitude. The sun beat down and I felt the beginnings of a headache.

"How far up is it?" The incline seemed endless. We'd left the rock climbers far behind. There were only us, the huge slope, and the vast, azure sky with the sun beating down like it was trying to bore a hole directly into my skull.

Stephen took a clean, folded bandanna from his pocket and

tipped some water onto it. Then he laid the cool, wet cloth on the back of my neck. It felt heavenly. "Just a couple more minutes," he said, his forehead creased with concern. "I'm sorry—I forgot how high we are."

I tied the bandanna's ends around my neck and took a big swig of my water. My headache backed off a couple notches. "I'm okay." I smiled at him.

"It's totally worth it. Here, check this out." He ducked behind me so that we were standing single file on the path with me in front.

Before I could ask what we were doing, I felt his hands pushing at my back.

"What . . . ?" I tried to turn around.

"Start walking," he instructed.

"You're crazy!" But when I did start walking, I almost fell over. It was like being carried up the hill. His strong arms pushed me as I walked, giving me an assist with every step. "This is awesome!" I laughed. "I'm going to have to take you everywhere with me."

"Or at least up every hill." He was deliciously close. Then he stopped. "Okay, check it out."

At first I could only see the last section of path. Then I turned around, and behind me was spread a panorama of snowy blue peaks rearing into the sky. I caught my breath. "So pretty," I breathed. "Wow." I inhaled the thin, cool air. It was as sweet as perfume.

We sat side by side on a sun-warmed boulder edged with

ruffled lichen, hands clasped around our knees, the wind blowing through our damp hair. "What's that one?" I pointed to a particularly craggy peak rearing up to the northwest.

Stephen squinted at it. "Pikes Peak—the tallest one in the Rockies." He fished a compass in a black case from his pocket. He clicked open the lid, which had a vertical slit in it. Then he leaned over and held it up. "Here, take a look."

I peered through the slit. "I only see the ground."

"Here." He edged behind me and put both arms over my shoulders so my back was to his front. I swallowed and tried to keep from falling off the mountain. He positioned the compass in front of me. "Can you see it now?"

The top of the peak was perfectly framed in the compass now. "Yes," I said faintly. He moved an inch closer. Bolts of electricity zinged through me. I swallowed. He still held up the compass, but we both knew neither of us was looking at it.

Then the sun slipped behind a cloud, darkening the landscape. He snapped the compass closed and stepped back. I knelt and fumbled with my shoelace until my face cooled off.

"Ready to head back down? It looks like rain—storms can come up pretty fast up here." Stephen reached a hand down, and I grasped it and pulled myself up.

He held my fingers a moment longer than usual. I could have spoken then, but I didn't. And he didn't either—just turned and started walking down the path.

Chapter ✎ Eight

Miguel smiled at me, his teeth impossibly white, as he shoveled scrambled eggs and toast onto my plate. "Ready for the hayride today?" he asked, his dark eyes twinkling above his neatly trimmed mustache.

I groaned theatrically, looking across the bench at Dana, who was hunched over a bowl of Rice Krispies. "Bring it on," she muttered, keeping her voice low. Jack and Sandra were poring over clipboards of papers at the other end of the table, muttering to each other over a big ledger.

Miguel stopped piling on the eggs and started spooning out fruit salad. "Miguel, that's good!" I protested, trying to slide my plate away.

"Need to build you up," he said. "You'll need your strength for the guests this morning."

"Yes, I will," I laughed as he disappeared back into the kitchen. "So what's the route?" I asked Dana, salting and peppering the creamy soft eggs.

She lifted her bowl and drained the milk at the bottom. "Usual," she said with her mouth full. "Out onto the road and up to the antelope site. The guests love seeing the antelope. Should be some big ones out there too."

After eating, we pushed back from the bench and took our dishes to the pass-through window, then walked together out into the clear mountain air. I inhaled. I thought I'd never get tired of smelling it. We took a shortcut across the grass to the back of the stable, near the riding arena.

"Hey, how was the hike with Stephen?" Dana asked. "I never got to ask you yesterday." She pulled her hair into a low ponytail as we walked.

"I know, who goes to bed at eight o'clock?" I teased her. "I couldn't believe you were asleep when I got back."

She looked sheepish. "I know, I know. These five a.m. herd roundups are getting to me." We could see Rick and Stephen now, hitching up Mark and Scott, the Belgian draft horses, to the big red-painted wagon.

Dana pulled me to a stop beside a big stand of juniper. It smelled like the gin my dad liked to drink in the evenings. "Well, how was it?" she asked again.

I smiled. "Really nice."

"Aw! Are you guys, like, an item now?" She bent down and

picked up a rosy, translucent pebble, rolling it between her fingers.

I felt a little flush creeping up the back of my neck. "I don't know. It was only one date. But . . ." Suddenly, I flashed on Zach's face, laughing in the kitchen. I shook my head and shoved the image away. I pulled a couple of juniper berries off the bush and crushed them in my palm. "We talked, he told me about his stress with Rick."

Dana nodded. "I knew there was tension going on there. You'd have to be blind not to." She paused. "I know there's something else, though. I can just tell on your face."

"Well . . . I made tortillas with Zach yesterday. And it was fun. He was being nice for once. You know, not teasing constantly." I let the berries drop and wiped my hands on the sides of my jeans.

"Oh my God, you have a crush on him too!" Dana's voice rose.

"Shh." I grabbed her arm and pulled her to a stop beside me. "No. It's not like that. I like Stephen; I told you. Zach was just—" I floundered around. "I don't know why I even mentioned it."

"Well, good." Dana started walking again. "Because Zach just seems kind of arrogant sometimes—Stephen is so sweet!"

"I know—they're so different. They were getting on each other's nerves in the barn a couple days ago, arguing about the horses."

Stephen looked up from Mark's harness, hearing our approach. He flashed us a heart-ripping smile, and Dana and I looked at each other significantly.

"Good morning, ladies," Stephen greeted us gallantly. He

looked especially adorable, wearing a blue T-shirt that showed off his pecs, with his auburn hair still wet from his shower.

Rick gave us the briefest of nods and went back to tightening one of the wagon's wheel bolts with a wrench. Mark and Scott already had their bridles on, and they slung their heads to look at us past their blinders. "Hey, boys." I patted their massive, arching necks, feeling the power in the muscles there. One of them could have easily swallowed my whole hand if he wanted to. But their eyes were gentle and calm, fringed with thick, beautiful blond eyelashes, as if they were equine mascara models. "Are you guys excited for the hayride?"

Scott bobbed his head as if replying. Dana went around the other side to help Rick with the wagon wheel. Stephen was bent over, inspecting Mark's front left hoof. He straightened up and flashed me a grin. "You all recovered from the hike yesterday?"

"Are you kidding? That was easy," I teased him. "You're the one who probably needs to recover." I grinned at him in the morning sunshine. "Is Mark's hoof okay?"

"Yeah, he's got a big stone. I've got to get a hoof pick."

"I'll get it." I walked toward the stable.

"Can you get the big one with the red rubber handle?" he called after me.

"Sure!" The stable was dim after the bright outdoors. I paused, giving my eyes a chance to adjust. In the tack room I scanned the wall of neatly hung grooming tools: scrapers and currycombs and mane combs and bottles of tail detangler and rags for wiping eyes and little squeegees for squeezing the water out of furry coats after a bath, which always reminded me of the squeegees at gas stations for cleaning your windshield. There were all kinds of hoof picks, but I couldn't find the big red one.

I crossed to the feed-room door on the opposite wall. Maybe someone had left it in there. I opened the door and stopped. Zach stood with his back to me, a feed scoop lying on the closed grain bin beside him and a canvas bag crumbled in one hand. He'd obviously been getting Mark and Scott's lunch ready for the trip, but now his hands were braced on the windowsill and his head was bowed. His shoulders were hunched and shaking a little. I realized he was crying.

"Zach?" I whispered, almost dumbstruck. It was like witnessing a tornado or some kind of freak storm.

He whirled around at the sound of my voice, and involuntarily I took a step back. His eyes were red and his cheeks were wet. He quickly turned his back to me and swiped rapidly at his cheeks.

"What do you want?" he snapped, prying the lid off the grain bin and rapidly scooping out corn.

"I, um, was looking for the big hoof pick." I cleared my throat. "Um, are you okay?" I thought about laying a hand on his back, but didn't move.

He dropped the scoop in the bin and pressed the lid back on, then gathered up the canvas bag and pushed past me without meeting my eyes. The door clapped closed behind him.

For a long moment I just stood there. Then I saw a scrap of

paper lying on the floor by the bins. I bent down and picked it up. It was a photo, folded over and stained in several places, the edges curled. Slowly I unfolded it, smoothing out the creases with my fingers.

It showed Zach and another boy, a little older, bent over a barbecue on a patio, half grinning over their shoulders at the camera. Sausages and slabs of zucchini were arrayed before them on the grill. It must have been summer, because they were both tanned. Zach wore a ball cap, his hair fluffing out beneath it, and the other boy was shirtless. I looked closely at his face—he had the same ice-blue eyes and black hair, the same cheekbones. It had to be his brother, Dan.

I turned the photo over and over in my hands. Zach must have dropped it. Had he been in here alone, looking at it? I pushed the feed-room door open and passed through the tack room, then the stable, back into the sun.

Dana and Rick were at the back of the wagon with the backboard lowered, pitching clean straw into the back for the guests to sit on. The freshness was beginning to wear off the morning. From the guest cabins to the west, I could hear faint voices and doors slamming. It was almost time to leave. Stephen looked up from the strap he was adjusting on Scott's bridle. "Did you find it?"

I looked toward Zach, who was leaning against the wagon, his hands stuffed in his pockets. He glanced at me, looking supremely unconcerned. Any trace of what had happened in the feed room was gone.

Stephen cleared his throat expectantly.

"I, ah—hang on." I hurried over to Zach and dug my hand in my pocket. "Zach, hey, did you drop—"

But before I could get any more words out, he held up the red hoof pick. "Looking for this?" he asked. His voice held the same merry, careless tone I knew so well.

"Yes, Stephen wants it for Mark's foot. He has a stone." I felt discombobulated, as if someone had twirled me around with my eyes closed and then let me go. I reached my hand out for the pick, but he held it just out of my reach. "Zach!"

"What's it worth to you?" He grinned and held the pick a little higher.

"Give me that." I swiped at it. He was teasing, of course.

"You're so cute when you're mad." His eyes danced.

I resisted the urge to bite him, like I was still in preschool. Instead I lunged forward and grabbed his arm. After a brief tussle, I managed to wrench it from his hand.

"There." I pushed my hair back from my face, trying to catch my breath. "You are the biggest pain." I turned to go.

"You love it!" he called after me.

I stomped over to Mark without looking back and pulled at the blond, feathery fur around his hoof, pressing my shoulder into his warm flesh. I supported the smooth hard horn in my left hand, bent at the waist, taking care that my feet were to the side, out of the way in case the hoof slipped or he stamped it down. Dana had shown me the blue rings on her toenails from getting stomped. I picked fast, cleaning dirt and matted manure out from his hoof. I could see the tip of the big stone, but it was buried in other debris.

Mark's hoof seemed to weigh a thousand pounds. My wrist was aching. I jammed the hoof pick against the stone.

"I like that view."

Zach was behind me again. I could see him upside down from my distinctly compromising position, bent double with my bottom sticking out.

"Don't be a douche." Stephen stepped into my field of view.

Zach's brow grew stormy. "Shut up, Steve. I'll be a douche if I want."

I pushed hard against the hoof pick, and the stone flipped out of the hoof with a clink on the ground.

With relief, I gently set Mark's hoof down and straightened up, yanking up the back of my jeans at the same time. "Thanks for defending my honor," I told Stephen, eyeing Zach, who grinned and shoved his hands in his pockets, strolling away.

"A waaggooonn!"

Miriam, the oldest of the snarly-haired, out-of-control daughters, zoomed toward us, trailing her equally snarly-haired yet whinier sister, August.

"Hang on!" Dana swiped at them, managing to catch August around the middle like she was a stray calf, but Miriam slipped by her, making a beeline for Mark and Scott.

"Girls!" I called. "Miriam! Stop! Remember what I told you about running around the horses?"

Rick straightened up and gave me a look I could easily read. It said, *Get these children under control before they hurt themselves or one of the horses.*

Miriam was now climbing up the back of the wagon like a chimp, totally crazed, as if she'd been given meth that morning instead of Cheerios.

"Okay, down you go." Zach reached over the edge and lifted her up bodily, hanging on to her around the waist. She let out a screech like a girl in a slasher film. Zach lifted her over the wagon wheel as if she were a sack of grain and offered her to Stephen.

"Oh no, man, don't stick her with me." He raised his hands and backed away.

"Where's her mom?" I looked down the path toward the cabins. As usual, she was walking up the path, chatting to Mrs. Coleman, totally oblivious to her own children and more than happy to let us do the work of not keeping them from killing themselves or someone else.

Zach didn't answer. He was examining the strap Stephen had been adjusting on Scott's bridle. "This is cracked, dude," he said. "It's going to split."

Stephen's brow immediately darkened. He leaned over to look at it. "It's fine." He turned away.

Zach shrugged. "It's not. But that's cool—you just keep telling yourself that." He picked at his teeth with a thumbnail.

Stephen faced Zach, looking stormy. "What are you saying?

That I don't know what I'm doing?" He was getting red, and I could see a vein popping out on his neck.

Zach just gazed back at him calmly.

I looked from one to the other like I was at Wimbledon, but before anyone could speak, Rick slammed the backboard shut with a thump. We were ready to go.

We all loaded onto the wagon: Dana on the seat, Rick at the reins, with me and the two boys in the straw at the back with the Taylors and poor, sad little Mrs. Coleman. She looked even worse today, with gray circles under her eyes and uncertain strands of hair wavering around her head. When I got close to her to help her into the wagon, I smelled stale wine on her breath.

I settled in a corner as close to Stephen as I could get and hung on to the back of August's shirt, since she kept leaning out of the wagon to grab at nearby branches. "I'm trying to catch a squirrel," she insisted when I told her to stop.

"Stop, August," the dad said in his defeated way.

Rick clucked to the horses and they leaned into the harness. The wheels turned and the wagon creaked its way down the long driveway.

As we turned right onto the dirt road that wove its way back into the outer reaches of the ranch, Stephen took my guitar from the straw. He'd asked to borrow it before we left. He played a few tunes, and when he got to "Danny Boy," Mrs. Coleman surprised us all by chiming in with a reedy soprano. She looked almost invigorated when we were through, despite the fact that "Danny Boy" gets a prize for being the world's saddest song.

I alternated between keeping the kids from throwing hay at each other and the horses and keeping an eye on Zach and Stephen, who were still glowering from opposite corners, though neither of them was speaking. That was good.

The horses pulled harder against their harnesses, and the wagon tilted upward. We had left the dirt road behind. Now only two wagon ruts marked the sunny grass slope. I looked down and saw a rushing mountain brook below a steep bank. Pine trees and boulders littered the shores, as if a giant had broken his toys, then wandered away, leaving them behind.

"Whoa." Rick twitched the reins, and Mark and Scott obediently came to a halt. "Here we are."

We had stopped in a little glade of aspen trees, arranged in almost a perfect circle set back from the edge of the brook. Some rough lengths of logs were turned upright to form crude seats. The rustling leaves cast a cool green light over us, a welcome respite from the glare of the sun, which was now high in the sky.

Dana jumped down from the wagon seat and began unloading gear for the picnic lunch. Stephen reached out around the wagon box and unfastened the backboard. As soon as he lowered it, I let go of August's shirt, and she and Miriam shot out of the wagon like they were in a slingshot. Their parents followed at a leisurely pace, the mother looking at her phone, the dad staring glumly at his two daughters, who were now fighting over one of the log seats. Dana offered her hand to Mrs. Coleman, who delicately picked her way through the straw and down to the ground, where she immediately walked over to the brook and stared down into its burbling depths.

Zach jumped down and turned to me. "Here." He offered me his hand.

"Thanks." I hopped to the ground and looked around for Stephen, expecting him to have also been ready to help me down, especially since he was the one I really wanted. But he was already at the front of the wagon beside his brother. Rick was talking to him in a low, intense voice. He was holding a broken strap of leather in his hand and shaking it almost in Stephen's face. Stephen was looking down at the ground, mumbling. His cheeks were pink and his shoulders looked stiff. The strap had split after all. I darted a glance at Zach, half hoping he had missed what was happening. He hadn't. As I watched, Stephen glanced over at him, and Zach gave Stephen a big cheese-eating grin. Stephen looked like he wanted to sock him.

I went over to help Dana unload the lunch. "This place is so pretty. But I don't see any antelope."

She gestured to the open land just beyond the grove. "They're usually out there. They take off when they hear us, but they'll wander back."

"What food did Miguel pack?"

"Let's see." She pulled out a foil-wrapped packet of tortillas and a giant tub of what looked like chili. "We're going to make a fire and heat the chili over the flames. The guests love it, and Rick gets to show off his fire skills," she told me. "Hey, do you mind getting some wood? Just whatever's on the ground."

"Sure." I wandered away among the trees, scanning for fallen branches until the sounds of the picnic receded behind me. All around was only the soft rustle of the aspen leaves and, faintly, the distant scream of a hawk. I gathered a handful of twigs and then a couple of medium-sized branches. My hands were getting full. I bent to pick up one more branch, when I heard the crack of twigs behind me. I turned around to see Zach coming through the trees, looking like some kind of modern-day Robin Hood. "Hey. I didn't know you were back here."

"Just getting wood." Only then did I notice his hands were full of branches too.

"Those little twigs?" I teased. "You call that wood?"

He raised his eyebrows, smiling a little. "Oh, I see how it is, McKinley. You've got some pretty pathetic wood there yourself."

"That's all I could find!" I protested. "It's not like I'm in here toting an ax."

A devilish light I'd grown to recognize started in Zach's eyes. He looked up, scanning the nearby trees. "There. How about that for wood?"

I followed his gaze. A large branch about as big around as my arm was dangling from an oak tree, suspended only by a thin strip of bark. It was partially propped on another large branch, keeping it from falling to the ground. "What about it? It's like twenty feet up!"

Dramatically, Zach opened his arms and let all the wood he was holding fall to the ground. "I'm getting it."

"Are you part chimp? You're seriously going to climb up that tree?"

"If I do, will you go out with me?" He spoke lightly, but I sensed a serious undercurrent behind his voice. I flushed, glad he was facing away from me now, apparently evaluating the tree trunk for the best plan of attack.

"I don't know . . . ," I said softly, but he wasn't listening—at least, I don't think he was. I felt like I was being disloyal to Stephen somehow, just by answering, even though we weren't technically together.

Zach leaped at the tree like a cat and landed several feet up, clinging to the trunk with both arms and legs wrapped around it. Just as fast, he fell off, landing on the ground with a thud. "Ow."

I laughed. "So smooth."

He jumped to his feet, bits of bark clinging to his shirt. "I just need to try that again." This time he launched himself at the trunk harder and immediately rebounded onto the ground. "Ahh." He held his hand to his face.

"Zach!" I knelt beside him. His nose was bleeding a little, and he had a small cut above his lip. "Seriously, stop! You're crazy, you know that?"

"We need firewood—it's an emergency." His voice had a faint honking quality with his hand over his nose. "If we don't cook lunch, the Taylor girls are going to cannibalize their parents."

I guffawed. "We can't let that happen." I stood up, brushing off my knees, and circled the tree, looking up at it carefully.

"Hey, now!" Zach sat up. "Who's the crazy one?"

"Definitely still you," I said, and jumped to reach the lowest branch on the trunk. I just snagged it and, wiggling around to get a better grip, kicked my legs back and forth until I had enough momentum to swing them up and over the branch.

"If you kill yourself, I don't think Jack will let me keep working here," Zach called up to me.

I didn't answer—I was concentrating on pulling myself up until I could stand upright on the thick bottom branch. I steadied myself with a thinner branch just overhead, and looked down at Zach through the scrim of green leaves. Light danced across his handsome, high-cheekboned face as he gazed up at me. "Hi, down there."

"Hi. Were you raised by monkeys and just haven't told me yet?"

"Maybe." I started edging along the branch toward the dangling firewood. "I used to climb our mulberry tree every afternoon with my friend Jess. It was the best reading tree." I swiped at the dangling branch and wobbled.

"Easy, cowboy!" Zach called up.

"I've almost got it." The branch was tantalizingly in reach. Just another step, and one little yank . . . "Got it!" I let the branch fall through the leaves and crash to the ground.

I crouched down and, balancing with one hand, sat on the big branch, then swung my legs over and, clasping it with both arms, lowered myself off. Holding on, my legs dangling, I looked down. The ground looked farther away than I remembered it. Zach must have seen the hesitation in my face.

"Here, I'll break your fall." He reached his arms up.

"I'll squash you!" I squealed just as my sweaty hands began to slip.

I landed on him with a thump, and we both hit the ground, with me lying on top of him. "Oh God, are you okay?" I laughed and at the same time realized that our faces were only inches away. I could feel his heart beating through his shirt. My own breath stopped. His eyes dropped to my lips, and suddenly I knew, *knew*, he was going to kiss me. All motion stopped. The whole world narrowed down to his mouth so close to mine. My mind spun, gabbling questions, instructions, but my body and my breath were still.

"Where's the firewood?"

I jumped as if Zach had turned into a red-hot poker and rolled off him, scrambling to my feet. Dana stood a few feet away, a wad of crumpled newspaper in her hand.

"What—fire—firewood?" I stuttered, feeling my face flaming.

Dana looked like she was suppressing laughter. "Sorry, did you get distracted?"

"Dude, we totally have the wood right here," Zach broke in smoothly, and pushed past us with the big branch. "I'll chop it up." He shot me one backward smile, then disappeared through the trees.

Dana turned to me with both eyebrows raised so high I thought they were going to fly off her forehead.

I waved my hands in front of my face to ward her off. "Don't. Just . . . don't. I have no idea what that was, so don't even ask me."

She grinned. "It looked pretty obvious what that was to me—"

"Just dumb messing around." I cut her off, taking the newspaper out of her hand. "Is this for tinder? I'll go find the matches." I turned and walked unsteadily back toward the camp, forgetting all the wood I was supposed to have been collecting.

I sank thankfully into my creaky bed later that night. Dana was already snoring faintly across the room. The moonlight laid its cool path across the scratchy wool blanket, and outside the open window the dry grass rustled in the wind. Even fainter than that was the stamp and rattle of the horses at the hay rack in the pasture. I closed my eyes and crooked my arm over my face, feeling each weary muscle loosening, sinking down into the mattress. Slow swirls of sleep moved over me already, taking me away. Drowsily I kicked my dirty jeans off the end of the bed. They slid to the floor, and something fell out of the pocket with a faint click.

My mind woke up a few degrees and I leaned over the bed and dragged the jeans toward me. It was Zach's photo that had fallen out of the pocket.

Easing myself back onto my pillow, I unfolded the stiff paper once again. I tilted it slightly so that the moonlight from the window illuminated the faces of the younger Zach and his brother.

I studied it carefully—their ruddy, grinning faces looking back over their shoulders at the camera. Zach held a wooden-handled spatula. But it was Dan's hands that captivated me: long fingers, bony knuckles, neat fingernails. I'd seen almost identical hands earlier today, clasping mine as I lay so close to Zach after my tumble from the tree.

Chapter 9

"All right, get along!" Dana called, riding easily on Sunny, her palomino mare. She squeezed the horse to a jog, moving close to Mrs. Coleman, who was bouncing helplessly in her saddle, clutching the horn with both hands. At the back of the group, one of the Taylor girls was crying again, while the father tried to comfort her in his usual desperate, placating whisper. The oblivious mother rode up front, peppering Rick with questions about the sustainability of the ranch's water supply, and I brought up the rear on Magic.

All three of the new horses had made a lot of progress, but Magic had made even more progress than I thought he would. He would let me and Zach put on his halter and bridle, as long as we worked slowly and carefully and didn't touch his ears any more than absolutely necessary. He still wouldn't let Stephen near him, though—not since that first day when Rick had made Stephen tie him up. Stephen said he wasn't worried, but I didn't believe him. And the tension in his hands and voice whenever he came near Magic now just made the horse avoid him more. He'd even tried to bite Stephen the other day, and Zach had laughed, which hadn't helped the situation.

The water problem was the worst, though—every time I filled his bucket with the hose, he rolled his eyes and stood in the very back corner of his stall, as far away from the hose as possible. And he wouldn't drink at all from the big trough in the pasture if a hose was filling it up at the same time. But as soon as the surface of the water was calm, he relaxed.

Now I ran my hand up and down his beautiful gray-brown fur and guided him with the other. His mouth was beautifully responsive—the slightest twitch of my fingers and he pricked up his ears, waiting to see what I was asking. Even his trot was smooth, jostling me just slightly in the saddle.

Dana led the group through one of the main pastures. "This way, everyone!" she called, waving us to follow her. She squeezed Sunny into a slow lope, and with varying degrees of competency, the guests followed in a straggling line.

I asked Magic for a canter and he picked it up easily while I relaxed, enjoying the rocking motion of his lovely gait, admiring the way the dry, yellow grass contrasted almost violently with the jewel-blue sky.

The path twisted and meandered, carrying us up and down

little hills. I pressed my heels down further, trying to imagine my legs as long lines clinging to Magic's sides without gripping, as my old riding teacher used to say. Then a small burbling creek appeared in my peripheral vision, and the path dipped and turned until it was running parallel.

Magic pulled up suddenly, almost rocking back on his legs. I gasped and gripped the reins, struggling to keep from falling forward onto his neck, and quickly scanned the path for snakes, by far the most common cause of spooking out here.

The path was clear, though, and still Magic veered away as if repelled by an invisible magnet. Automatically, I tried to steer him back, but he raised his head high, trying to avoid the bit, and broke into a fast, bouncing trot.

"It's the creek, isn't it, boy?" I murmured. I steered him off the trail, managing to slow him down. I walked him in a large circle, stroking his neck.

"Hey, Chloe, are you okay?" Dana yelled back. She'd pulled up, and the group was waiting for me, twisted around, staring back.

"Yeah, I'm fine," I called.

"Well, come on! We're all supposed to stay together." She turned back around in her saddle and started Sunny at a walk. "All right, everyone!" she shouted back to the group. "We're going to cross this little creek. It's only up to the horses' ankles, so don't worry!"

A little ripple of excitement ran through the group as first

Sunny, then the others, carefully picked their way down a sloping little bank and across the burbling creek. I tried to steer Magic to follow, but he kept veering away from the creek. "Come on, boy, this is the crossing," I murmured to him. "I know you're afraid, but we have to do it." My shoulders were starting to ache with the effort of keeping him on the path, and I could tell he was agitated. The sides of his neck were dark with sweat, and the leather reins carved it off in foamy streaks. He was breathing heavily and snorting through his nostrils, slinging his head to avoid the bit. I could feel him wanting to turn—only the insistence of my legs and the pressure of the bit kept him moving forward.

"Come on, boy!" I urged him forward at the crossing and dug my heels into his sides, leaning forward in the saddle, my rein hand far up his neck, moving him forward. Still he veered away.

I pressed my heels into his sides so that he couldn't get away from the pressure and twirled the long ends of the reins in my free hand, catching him lightly on the flank. Big mistake. He flung up his head, almost hitting me in the face as I leaned forward, and wheeled around. I lurched to the side, clutching the horn in an attempt to regain my balance, feeling my right foot slip from the stirrup, the reins flapping. His strong muscles bunched underneath me, and I felt him pick up speed alarmingly fast.

We pounded away from the creek, me almost hanging off his side, feeling the saddle slip too, though I'd tightened the cinch as far as it would go before I mounted.

Ground and sky rushed at me dizzily tilted, and fleetingly I prayed, *Please don't let him step in a hole.* I clutched at mane, reins, saddle. Faintly, from somewhere behind me, I heard Dana's voice yelling, "Sit up! Sit up! Pull back!"

I'm trying, I said to her in my mind, but it was no good. I thumped to the ground, jarring my side and landing painfully on my ankle. I pushed myself up just in time to see my horse disappearing over the horizon.

"It's a water phobia," I said three hours later, sitting on one of the old couches in the common room with Dana, Stephen, and Zach around me. My foot was propped on a chair. Stephen sat close next to me, and every now and then he reached over and solicitously rearranged the bag of frozen peas that sat on my ankle. Sandra had inspected me closely after Dana brought me in all dirty, and had sat me here on the sofa with strict instructions to ice my ankle for an hour.

"He was doing so great until we hit the creek," I went on. Dana nodded thoughtfully.

"He was totally scared. I could see it in the way he was refusing you." She hitched her foot up on the sofa arm and rested her chin on her knee. "You did great staying on as long as you did."

"Nice job." Stephen patted my knee and smiled.

Dana went on. "He's been through a lot. Someone probably forced him through a creek or a river when he was younger. He could've lost his footing or was carrying too heavy of a rider."

"And couldn't swim?" I shuddered, thinking of Magic frightened and struggling in the middle of a river somewhere.

"Your pony's back," Rick said from the doorway. He tromped over and pulled out one of the creaky wooden chairs, collapsing into it. The chair squeaked a protest. "Showed up at the stable door just a few minutes ago. Jack's checking him over now, but he looks okay."

I breathed a sigh of relief. But it was short-lived. Anxiety seized me when Rick fixed me with his hard stare. "You got an explanation for this?"

I told him what happened, as briefly and clearly as I could.

The room was silent when I finished. My stomach was sick. I couldn't look at the boys. Then from beside me, I felt Dana's foot give mine a little kick. It gave me the courage to look Rick in the face. His mouth was a hard line. He looked at me, Stephen, and Zach each in turn. "We kept that horse after you kids told us you'd work on him. Now he's gone and spooked. We can't trust him with a guest as of now." Rick shoved his chair back with a scrape and stood up, his leather belt creaking under the weight of his belly. "Jack's given you all another chance to get him ready for the pack trip." He looked directly at Stephen. "I don't know why. That horse is better off as meat."

He clumped out of the room, the heels of his boots thumping the worn boards.

We all sat in silence. I felt sick. Magic had another chance, but barely. He could not screw up again.

Stephen sat with his head bowed, his forearms resting on his knees. His hair obscured his face. He didn't look at anyone. "It's my fault." His voice was muffled.

"What?" Dana asked.

He raised his face. The freckles stood out in bright blotches. "He should've been ready by now. I should have considered the water issue." He smacked his knee with his fist, and we all jumped. "It's okay." His voice was tight. It was clear that it wasn't okay. "He'll be ready for the pack trip. I'll make sure he is."

We all stared at him, mouths open. I could feel the intensity radiating off him, beating against me like heat from a fire.

"Of course he'll be ready," I said gently. "We'll all work with him." I glanced quickly at Zach, but he was watching Stephen, his eyes narrowed.

Stephen shook his head. "He's my responsibility. It's my head if he spooks again."

This time no one argued with him. He was right.

Chapter • Ten

The air was damp and fresh when I tiptoed out of the bunkhouse at dawn, holding my boots in one hand. For once, I'd beaten Dana out of bed. She was still a rumpled hump under her covers, sleep mask firmly in place. She had the morning off and had declared the night before that she was going to sleep until noon.

I paused and tugged on my boots. The sunrise was turning the sky a deep rose red, with streaks of purple and lavender, with the mountains a bumpy black silhouette and the last of the night stars fading in the western sky. I'd agreed to meet Stephen for an early Magic session, though he hadn't told me just what he had in mind. The last two weeks had been tense. Stephen just couldn't seem to connect with Magic, and the horse tried to bite him whenever he came near. It didn't help that Magic would let

Zach tack him up and ride him. I tried not to notice how hard Stephen's hands were and how tense his body was whenever he handled Magic. The horse was picking up on Stephen's desperation. They always did.

I sniffed as I stood up from the porch. Pancakes. I was missing breakfast. Reluctantly, I climbed down from my rock, peeling the wrapper off the granola bar I'd stuffed into my pocket on the way out.

When I got to the stable, Stephen already had Magic out on a lead rope. He was leaning back against the fence, waiting for me, apparently. The golden morning sun glinted on his auburn hair, and he was wearing a soft gray plaid shirt, open just enough at the collar for me to admire the burnished gold of his skin. I didn't ask if Magic had tried to bite. It seemed better not to, especially when I saw Stephen's face. He was bursting with something, I could tell.

"I thought we'd try him out on a creek," Stephen called when he saw me. He turned around almost immediately as I came up, and I hurried after him as he started to lead Magic across the field.

"Don't you think it's a little early to be trying him on water again?" I stumbled over tough tussocks of grass, trying to keep up. I cast a hasty glance around for Zach. Stephen was too worked up to handle Magic right now.

Stephen stopped and handed me the lead rope. "Can you hold him a sec? I've got a rock in my boot." He bent down and tugged at his boot as I looked again toward the stable. Maybe if I just dawdled enough . . .

Stephen tugged at his boot. "Here, do you need help?" I offered.

"I got it." He pulled it off, exposing a forest-green sock with a hole in the big toe, and dumped out a small pebble. "There."

I kept my eyes fixed on the pasture gate. A figure with black hair appeared around the corner of the stable, and I breathed an imperceptible sigh of relief. Zach caught sight of us, and his steps quickened as he headed purposefully for the pasture.

Stephen had just pulled on his boot and stamped his foot on the ground when Zach came up.

"Hey, what's up?" he greeted us. He eyed Magic on the lead line. "You're taking him to the creek already? Don't you think it's a little early for that?"

Stephen's brow darkened. I could practically see him grow bristly before my eyes. "No, obviously I don't, or I wouldn't be doing it," he retorted. He pushed past Zach with Magic. "Let's keep going," he said to me over his shoulder.

I threw a quick glance at Zach, who grinned and shrugged. I turned and hurried after Stephen. It was a slow, sullen trip across the pasture to the bottom, where a small creek meandered through the grass before flowing into the aspen grove at the other end. The icy waters ran over the grass, wetting it, releasing a delicious peaty smell into the air.

As we walked across the pasture, I stepped to the side of one of the hillocky tufts of grass and came down hard on the side of my ankle, still sore from the fall. I hissed involuntarily and reached down to grab my leg with both hands.

"You okay?" I looked up to see Zach beside me. Ahead, Stephen was still walking with Magic. He must not have heard me.

"I'm fine." I forced myself to stand up and gritted my teeth at the sharp ache in my ankle.

Zach's big hand was under my elbow. I looked up into his icy-pale eyes, which pierced right into mine. His fingers were strong and warm on my elbow. "This is going to be a disaster," he murmured.

"It'll be fine," I said with a conviction I was far from feeling. "Stephen knows all about horses." I sensed Zach knew I was just mouthing the words.

He looked amused. "That's not how I would put it, exactly. Are you going to the dance tonight?"

"Yeah, of course." He was talking about the big ranch square dance, the send-off for the pack trip. Everyone from all the sections of the ranch would come together to dance out under the stars, and then two days later, we'd all leave for the pack trip in our various sections. Our section was going to Durango Falls. It was a full day's ride out; then we'd spend the night and head back the next day, arriving at the ranch the following night. All the guests were excited about the dance and the trip—none of them had ever spent a night outdoors with the horses before.

Zach released my elbow. "Okay, just checking."

We stopped at the banks of the creek. Magic was sniffing the air, his ears already pricked with apprehension. "There, boy," I crooned, stroking his neck. Sweat was tracing dark rivulets down his chest, making him smell like a wet wool sweater. "It's going to be okay. Don't be afraid." I splashed my hand in the water and showed it to him. "Look, see? Just water."

He dipped his head and snuffled at my hand, his eyes large and his nostrils twitching.

"All right, so Chloe, you get on one side of the halter, and I'll get the other. Zach, you get behind him and give him a good whack on the flanks. I brought this." Stephen reached into his back pocket and produced a short brown riding crop.

I hesitated. "Um, Stephen—"

Zach broke in. "Okay, first of all, who made you the boss? Second, I can guarantee you that horse is going to flip out if you force him across. He's totally not ready for that." He faced Stephen across the horse's back.

"Who says he's not ready? *You?* I'm sorry, but I've been around horses my entire life." Stephen was getting red in the face. "You just got here for the summer, bro."

Zach shrugged. "Whatever. Find out for yourself." A lazy, dangerous light was glinting deep in his eyes. I swallowed, looking from one boy to the other. Some instinct told me to keep quiet.

Stephen eyed Zach and then seemed to come to a conclusion in his head. "Okay, fine. Chloe, get his head. Zach, you—"

Zach shook his head. "That's where you're wrong, bro. You're on your own."

Stephen stared at him, then took a firm hold on the lead rope. "Chloe, you get the other side."

I felt a momentary rebelliousness at his presumptuous tone, but shrugged it off. He *did* know a lot about horses. Still, something in my heart told me that Zach was right, Magic wasn't ready, and he should be brought along more slowly.

But Stephen was already holding the halter on one side, looking at me expectantly. Reluctantly, I took hold of the other side. Stephen tugged on the lead rope, but I could tell immediately that there was no way the horse was going to move.

"Come on, boy!" Stephen urged. Magic planted his hooves and threw up his head, snorting. Stephen pulled harder and then smacked the horse on the flank with the loose end of the lead rope. Magic flattened his ears, whipping his head back and forth.

"Stephen, I'm not sure—" I said, placing my hand on his arm. The muscles beneath my palm were as hard as wires.

"I've got him," he panted. "Get up, boy!"

I knew that the only way anyone would get Magic to cross the stream was to pull hard on his head, one person on each side, while someone else beat him with a crop on the flanks. He'd go forward to get away from the crop and cross the stream, but this was so clearly the wrong idea I couldn't even believe Stephen was suggesting it. All that would do was make Magic even more afraid of the water—*and* he wouldn't trust us anymore. He'd never let anyone who did that to him get within ten feet of him.

"He's not ready, Stephen!" I insisted. "Please, seriously, don't force him."

"He can do it," Stephen said soothingly to me. "I know he's ready; we've been working with him."

"He's not!" Zach almost yelled. I'd never seen him get visibly angry. He leaned forward until he was right up in Stephen's face. "You jerk, you're just thinking about your stupid promotion, but this horse is *not ready*." He drew out the last two words with dangerous slowness.

Stephen's fists clenched, and for a minute I thought he was going to punch Zach. Instead he wheeled around and grabbed Magic's lead rope. "Come on, get up," he said roughly to the horse and, ignoring Magic's up-flung head, trotted him, snorting and pulling back, into and across the stream so fast I don't think the horse had time to think about it.

"There." Stephen looked at us from the other side, the panting, sweating horse, beside him. "He did it."

But no one was cheering. Zach's eyes met mine. *It* was *a disaster*, I said silently back. *You were right*.

Chapter ● Eleven

"I'm so excited!" I squealed that evening. My room was littered with clothes draped over the beds, flung on the floor. The closet door hung open, with empty hangers scattered everywhere. My flatiron and Dana's blow-dryer were perched precariously on the dresser.

"I think this is going to set those T-shirts on fire." I gingerly picked up the flatiron and clicked it off. "What do you think, straight or wavy?" I displayed the opposite sides of my head to Dana.

"Straight, definitely." She was applying eyeliner, leaning over the tiny spotted mirror propped on her bedside table and stretching the skin of her eyelid out taut. "Is Stephen coming by for you?"

I picked the flatiron up and clicked it on again, then opened and closed it a couple times, clacking the metal plates together.

"I told him I'd meet him there." I carefully closed the iron on a section of hair and drew it downward, listening to it hiss.

Preparations for the dance had been going on all week. Rick and Jack, with the help of Todd, Jeremy, and Chris, the wranglers, had laid a beautiful wooden temporary floor right on the short-mowed grass near the main house. Stephen had explained that you needed a hard surface for square dancing so that people's feet could make a loud noise when they stomped them down.

I'd always associated square dancing with insanely dorky yee-hawing in the school gym when we were forced to learn it in fourth grade. But out here it seemed like that was just the way people danced.

Mrs. Coleman even seemed excited—she was talking to me during her riding lesson about how she used to take Arthur Murray with her late husband. I didn't know what Arthur Murray was until Dana told me it was ballroom dancing, like the fox-trot, with dresses and tuxedos. Dancing on boards in the middle of a ranch sounded pretty different, but heck, whatever made her smile was good.

Despite my excitement, I did feel a little nervous. I was having bad flashbacks to the various bar mitzvah dances I'd been subjected to in seventh grade. Charlie Myer wouldn't dance with me, which at the time felt truly traumatic.

"So, explain to me how this works?" I asked Dana as I finished ironing one side of my head and started on the other side.

She was sorting through a little silk sack of jewelry, holding different earrings up to her ears. "Well, there's a band and a caller for the guests, and they have the dance out on the floor. We're supposed to dance too. Jack hates it when people hang back on the sidelines."

"That sounds great." I was ready to banish the ghosts of my seventh-grade dances, and this seemed like the perfect place to do it.

Dana and I grabbed our room keys and clattered down the stairs and out into the dusky, sweet mountain night. The sunset flared its last light behind the peaks in the distance, and all was quiet around us, except for the faint sound of music coming from behind the main house. We detoured briefly through the stable so I could just say good night to Magic.

The long, low building was peaceful with its dusty horse scent and occasional rattle of a water bucket. Magic's head nodded sleepily over the half door of his stall. "Hey, boy." I patted his velvety nose and he opened his eyes a bit wider. I leaned over and kissed him on his broad, flat cheek. "Don't be bothered by the music tonight."

"They'll be fine." Dana steered me away from the horse by my elbow. "Come on, we're going to be late."

We went around the corner of the house. Masses of people were gathered there in scattered clumps, some standing around on the shiny board floor laid on the grass, some clustered near a long table that was loaded with food. I sniffed appreciatively at the scent of tamales that drifted over to me on the wind.

I didn't recognize most of the people, but that was because they were from different sections on the farm. A group of little boys was running around, chasing each other and yelling. Some parent types were holding drinks and looking on indulgently, while at one end of the dance floor a band was setting up. I spotted a bass, and a fiddle, and a banjo. My heart leaped a little at the thought of hearing live music after all this time. Jack was down near the band, holding a portable mike in one hand and talking with a tall, stringy man in a cowboy hat. He must be the caller Dana had told me about. She said he went around to ranches and farms all summer, calling dances.

Rick was standing by the food with his hands stuffed in his pockets, talking to Miguel. Then I spotted Stephen, who was in a cluster in the corner with a bunch of what looked like wranglers from the other sections. I could always tell the wranglers because they dressed super cowboy, with pegged jeans and big belt buckles and boots.

Stephen spotted us and waved. "Hi," I said as we walked over. The wranglers nodded.

"Hi." He seemed cooled off from our bad morning.

"What's up, guys?" a voice said behind me. Stephen scowled. I whipped around to see Zach, grinning and standing there with a cup in his hand. My heart gave a quick double thump. He was wearing a gray V-neck sweater over a white T-shirt and leather flip-flops. It was the first time I'd seen him wearing anything other than boots or sneakers. He had nice toes.

Zach nodded at me. "You clean up pretty nice, McKinley." One of the wranglers nodded agreement.

I felt the tips of my ears turn red. "Oh, well. Thanks."

He smiled easily and gave my shoulder a little squeeze. Stephen's scowl deepened.

An awkward silence fell in our little group. I sensed Dana looking from Stephen to Zach to me and back again. "Well!" she said after a minute. "I'm hungry. You think Jack will mind if we eat now?" Without waiting for a reply, she strolled toward the food table, trailed by the wranglers.

A burst of music started from the other end, and I looked over. "Ladies and gentlemen, please take your places for the four-square," the caller called in a deep western twang.

The guests shuffled excitedly into place, holding hands and trying to form the squares of four couples as the caller instructed them. Oh God. Who was I going to dance with? I looked around for Dana to rescue me, but before I could spot her, Stephen grabbed my hand in his. "Come on! This is a great dance." His hand was sticky, the way it had been that first day when we'd held hands on the driveway. My eyes found Zach, who grinned at me and leaned against a post, folding his arms across his chest.

Stephen led me to the center of the dance floor. I noticed the rest of the staff forming little squares also. The fiddle crashed and the banjo twanged into song. The music was infectious—I couldn't keep my feet still. Holding on to Stephen's sweaty hand,

I tried as best as I could to follow the nasal instructions the caller was calling out in time to the music.

The squares of people turned toward each other, bowing and then turning away. I tried to bow to my partner, left and right, like I was being instructed. I felt the twang of the music deep in my throat, and I was swept away by the foot-stomping harmony.

The caller blared out directions that sounded like a song in themselves, clapping his hands and stamping his feet until he was almost dancing up there too, sweating under the crude lights rigged up on long poles. All around me faces twirled. I swirled one way and then another, barely able to catch my breath. Stephen swung into my field of vision, laughing, and then I swung back to the pudgy middle-aged man with a mustache, who grabbed my hand and do-si-doed me with great seriousness. Across the bright crowded room, I glimpsed Dana in another square, dancing with one of the long, lean wranglers, and Zach, still lounging against one of the poles.

Then a new dance started, a reel, another dance I'd never done before. The dancers, following the caller's instructions, formed two lines down the center of the room, holding hands with the person across from them to form a long archway of arms. The couple at the end held hands and danced down through the archway to the other end, then back down the floor once more.

Laughing, sweating, the dancers broke apart and reorganized into the long lines. "Chloe!" Stephen beckoned me over, arranging us across from each other so we would be partners. I stood waiting, slightly breathless from the dancing. The square dance was turning out to be much more fun than I thought—it was banishing all the ghosts of bar mitzvahs past.

I grinned at Stephen. His face shone a little with perspiration, and his auburn hair stuck to his forehead. "Yee-haw," I called out, not caring how insanely dorky I sounded. I just felt good.

"Take your places!" the caller bawled, and the music crashed into rollicking strains. It felt very appropriate there under the stars, evoking the ghosts of cowboys and cattle herds. We all joined hands, which looked very cool—a long archway all made of arms, with every smiling, sweating face turned toward the first couple dancing their way down the center. One by one, each pair sashayed down the line with varying degrees of proficiency, but everyone was laughing at themselves and at each other. It was a nice feeling, all of us together, the parents and us, and the kids running around, like we were all one big group. Bit by bit, the line inched up. It was our turn. All the eyes turned to us—at least, that's how it felt—and Stephen looked at me and grinned, and I took a deep breath and smiled back. He reached out and grabbed my hand and whisked me down the aisle. I tried to sashay as well as the others and I felt encouraged with the clapping hands all around us from the watchers standing on the edges.

At the end of the aisle, though, just as Stephen and I separated, Zach suddenly appeared before me. He grinned and held his hand out. Without thinking, I let go of Stephen and grabbed Zach. We galloped back down the archway before I realized what I'd done.

"I knew you had some cowgirl in you, McKinley!" Zach shouted over the music. He pulled me toward him, his hands on my waist.

"What's happening here?" Stephen said from behind us. I whirled around to see him standing there with his hands on his hips. Guilt washed over me. I'd abandoned him.

"No—nothing," I stammered. "I—ah—"

"I was dancing with Chloe. She's here with me." Stephen's face was flushed bright red, his fists balled up.

A little flare of annoyance rose in my chest. "Actually, I'm here by myself."

The music ended and everyone applauded. Stephen looked around, seeming to get ahold of himself. The crowd was surging toward the food table, where the tamales were disappearing quickly. "Look, let's just get some food, okay?" I looked from Stephen to Zach and back again.

The rest of the night passed in a blur of dancing, eating, then dancing again. When I think back to that night now, a few images stand out: The look on Rick's face when Miriam Taylor got sick all over his shoes after eating half a cream pie. Dana and Jeremy the wrangler, who was built like a sunflower, giggling together in a corner, her face as happy and goofy as I'd ever seen it. Miguel and Nora dancing together behind the food table at the end of the night, gazing into each other's eyes. Mrs. Coleman standing with a man from one of the other sections, smiling—smiling!—at him and talking. I almost cried, I was so happy for her.

Later, much later, I found myself in the common room, sprawled on one of the couches, with my head pillowed on Dana's leg. Zach was there too and Stephen and a bunch of the wranglers and a couple of other girls who were guests in the western section. They weren't supposed to be here, technically, but I think the wranglers invited them, and who cared, anyway? We were all drowsy and giddy from the night, draped over the furniture, making stupid, half-asleep jokes and giggling at them. Two of the girls were stealing the wranglers' hats, which they never took off, and making a game of trying them on. Stephen had my guitar out and was lazily plucking the strings.

"I love Colorado," I said dreamily, stupidly, staring at the ceiling. "I want to marry Colorado."

Dana snorted a laugh, her head resting on the back of the sofa.

"Don't lie. You're homesick, McKinley," Zach said from the armchair next to us. "I've heard you crying into your pillow at night."

"Seriously?" one of the wranglers said, looking at me incredulously.

I threw a pillow at Zach. "Shut up, you liar. No," I said to the wrangler. "He just likes to make trouble. It's like his job."

A discordant twang startled us out of our half-asleep talk. One of the girls had the guitar and was trying to play "Mary Had a Little Lamb" but was just screwing it up over and over and giggling at her mistakes.

Zach winced. Then he saw me watching and rolled his eyes toward the girl. I giggled.

Dana spoke up. "Zach, play for us. We need a lullaby." She leaned forward and plucked the guitar from the girl's hand.

Zach's shoulders tensed. "Nah. Not tonight."

"Oh, come on," one of the girls urged. "Play!"

"Getting stage fright?" Stephen spoke casually, but I heard the challenge in his voice. He took the guitar from Dana and shoved it at Zach. I inhaled sharply.

Zach shoved the guitar back at Stephen. "I said no!" He almost shouted the last word into Stephen's face.

Silence dropped over the group, broken only by Zach's breathing. Everyone stared at him. I looked down at my hands. I could hear the refrigerator humming in the kitchen. I looked up and met Zach's eyes. *Breathe,* I tried to communicate. *You don't have to play.*

He looked away, then grabbed the guitar from Stephen's hands. Before anyone could react, he strummed out "Row, Row, Row Your Boat." "There. Happy?" he asked the group. He dropped the guitar on the sofa and left the room, letting the screen door bang behind him.

Everyone else had gone to bed when I slipped downstairs later that night. For two hours I'd lain awake, listening to Dana's regular, even breathing and watching the moonlight move slowly across the wall from the light switch to the closet door.

Thinking of Zach's dark face over the guitar, the brooding in his eyes.

I couldn't remain still any longer. I slipped a hoodie over the tank top and striped pajama pants I'd worn to bed and softly padded down the stairs on bare feet. The room was dark with shadows.

The common room looked odd, deserted, lit only by the silvery light of the full moon outdoors. The furniture was still pushed around helter-skelter, the way we'd left it earlier, with the sagging couches and the scarred eating benches pushed against the walls. The guitar lay where Zach had dropped it.

The windows beside the couch were wide open, and as I sank down on the cushions, the secret night fragrance of pine and wood smoke came drifting in to circle around my head.

I picked up the guitar, laid it in my lap. The wood was smooth and cool. I plucked a string and a note fell into the silence like a raindrop on a still pond. I played a few more notes, moving up and down the strings, first slowly, then more quickly, only fumbling a little.

A melody flowed into my head and I played it. *Country roads, take me home, to the place, I belong, West Virginia, mountain mama, take me home, country roads.* I hummed the lilting lyrics as I swayed with the music. The song flowed through me and out of me, twisting and twining me in its magic until finally it was done.

I let my hands drop from the guitar in the silence.

A board creaked behind me, and I turned around to see a

dark figure stepping from the deep shadows in the corner.

It was Zach.

"What are you doing here?" My words came out hushed.

"Just chilling." His voice was a little thick.

"Were you spying on me?" I asked. I meant it as a joke, but he didn't respond.

"What's wrong?" I asked.

He paused. "I heard that song," he said quickly.

"I—I just felt like playing a little," I stumbled over my words. "I couldn't sleep." We were standing very close now. I wasn't quite sure how it happened, except I could feel the warmth from his body and smell the faint scent of peppermint on his breath.

We were both silent for so long, I started to feel awkward. "I—I like John Denver," I offered. I wondered how long we were going to stand here together in the dark.

He didn't respond.

"I'd forgotten that song until you played it at the campfire." I was babbling.

"Yeah." He cleared his throat. I wished I could see his face better. He picked my hand up and raised it to his mouth. My breath caught. His lips were hot and smooth when he pressed them to the back of my hand. An electric shiver went straight to my stomach.

"Well, good night," he said softly.

I tried to respond, but my voice wouldn't work. I tried again. "Good night," I managed.

While he watched, I trailed up the stairs. At the top, I stopped and looked down into the common room. He was still standing where I'd left him, his face tilted up to me but his expression hidden in shadows.

Chapter ☙ Twelve

The sunlight streamed through the little windows of the tack room the next morning, throwing into view the dust motes dancing everywhere. Dana was up on a box, tugging a saddle off a high rack. "Uh—ugh!" she grunted, yanking. The saddle came free and she swayed, trying not to fall backward from its weight.

"So, all these saddles have to get ready for the pack trip?" I asked, looking down at the clipboard resting on a box beside me. Jack had handed me the intimidating list this morning: twelve saddles, twelve bridles, fourteen halters, lead ropes, water buckets, bags of grain, flakes of hay. "How are we going to carry all this stuff?"

Dana hopped off the box, holding the dusty saddle in both arms. "This old behemoth weighs a ton. I don't think anyone's used it in ten years." She blew some dust off the seat. "We'll take pack horses and the mules. Some of the ranches just drive the gear up in a pickup a day before, but Jack likes the old-fashioned way, and the guests get a big kick out of it too. It's nice, everyone leaving together, leading the pack horses. Very old West."

She leaned the saddle on its horn against the wall, exposing the battered sheepskin underside, and hopped up on the box to tug another one down. "You're quiet this morning," she commented.

I looked at the bridle I was cleaning. I'd taken it to pieces, and now I was rhythmically soaping the damp old leather, watching each piece turn darker, dipping my little sponge in the basin of cloudy water, feeling the oily saddle soap on my fingers. "Yeah, well. I had another moment with Zach last night."

Dana's eyes lit up as she eased another saddle to the ground. "Oh yeah? You guys seem to be having a lot of moments recently."

"Yeah, I know." Briefly, I told her about Zach watching me in the common room and our confusing conversation afterward.

Dana listened, wrinkling her forehead. "So, are you into him? I thought you and Stephen were a thing." She draped the dusty saddle over a rack and with difficulty slid the buckles down from the stirrups.

"We never made that official." I swallowed, picturing Zach in the dark and the touch of his warm lips on the back of my hand. Dana wasn't looking at me, thank goodness. She was inspecting the stirrup she'd taken off the leathers.

"I think mice have been eating this," she remarked. "Does

Stephen know you two aren't official? We don't want any drama with the trip so close."

No drama. That's right. I bent my head to my soaping again.

"Are you excited for the trip?" I crooned to Magic later that day. "And you guys too," I added as the paint and the black crowded the bars. I snapped pieces off the carrot in my pocket and palmed a chunk each between their soft, whiskery lips. "It's going to be so much fun."

I unlatched the gate and stepped inside Magic's stall with the grooming box. He looked around at me and blew his breath through his nostrils. "There now," I crooned meaninglessly as I began grooming his tawny fur. The bare stripes were almost gone now, and he no longer jerked when I touched his head. In fact, he would let strangers pet him now, and last week when I accidently got his ear a little caught in his bridle, he didn't even shy away when I fixed it. It was just the water problem I was concerned about. The trial run across the creek had gone badly, in my opinion, though Stephen didn't seem to feel that way. Or maybe he wanted it to have gone better, so he was just hoping it would. I bent over and concentrated on scraping some mud from Magic's belly.

"That horse coming along there?" A gruff voice came from outside the aisle. I jerked upright.

Rick was standing outside the stall, holding a clipboard. His mustache looked especially bristly and aggressive today. Try as I might, I couldn't see any of Stephen in him.

"Yes, we've been working with him every day," I said. I always felt so intimidated, talking to Rick. "Stephen, especially."

He cast a cold eye up and down Magic. I encircled the horse's neck protectively, envisioning him on the auction block. "He better be. I've got—" He looked down at his clipboard. "I've got Linda Coleman riding him."

"Okay." What else could I say? Rick gave me a short nod and continued down the row of stalls. Dana had said there were several river crossings. I gulped and pushed that thought away. Magic would do fine. He just had to.

Everyone on the ranch gathered at sunrise the next morning. It was a thrilling sight in the fresh air, all of us spread out in front of the bunkhouse on the waving grass still thick with dew. Everyone was mounted—myself on Al, Stephen on Billy, Dana on her palomino that had come all the way from Idaho with her. Zach was riding Snickers, a big chestnut. There were four pack mules loaded with cookstoves, tents, sleeping bags, bags and boxes of food, ponchos, a first aid kit, even a flare gun in case we got lost or stuck in a mudslide.

The guests were all there too—the Taylor parents, each on their own horse. The little girls were each being ponied by a wrangler. And Mrs. Coleman on Magic. I had to keep my eyes from drifting constantly over to him. He looked beautiful in the dawn light, his fine head up, his eyes looking around calmly yet eagerly. But Stephen's eyes kept darting from Magic to his brother and back again. I could sense his tension from twenty feet away.

Jack sat before us on his big white gelding. "Friends and guests," he said, "we are about to embark on what will be the grandest adventure of your summer. For the next two days we will work together as a team. You will see some of the greatest scenery of your life. And, God willing, have some of the greatest adventures. And now . . . move out!" He waved his hat in the air and I could practically hear the thrilling fiddle strains as we all turned toward the rising sun and, with clopping hooves, little creaks of leather, and the jingle of gear, moved out of the ranch.

We spread out in an easy line as we headed off ranch property and began to climb a narrow, twisting path into the base of the mountain foothills. My fears about Magic began to diminish as we climbed the path. The sun crept steadily up in the sky, which turned from pearly pale blue-purple to a deeper, higher blue. I could feel my arms burning browner.

The horses' hooves crunched the stony dirt, kicking up dust in little puffs. Mrs. Coleman was in front of me on Magic, with Rick in front of them. Stephen rode just behind me, and Zach brought up the rear, as he'd been instructed. The Taylor girls were behaving for once, sitting slumped in their saddles, half-asleep in the warm morning sun. I was feeling a little drowsy myself, rocked by Al's rhythmic clopping and swaying, and the steady creaking of leather and jingling of metal that formed a soothing chorus around me.

"Don't fall asleep!" Zach's voice came from behind me, jerking me awake.

"You're not supposed to jump the line, rebel." I twisted around in my saddle. He rode straight and easy on his horse, his one hand easily controlling the reins, his other resting on his thigh.

"Couldn't stay back there. Everyone was going too slow."

I lowered my voice. "I'm nervous about Magic."

He squeezed his horse and rode up beside me. Our legs bumped. "He's totally quiet now. Mrs. Coleman's doing good controlling him." He gazed up the line at Magic's tawny haunches, then looked back at me. "I think he'll be fine at the water. Really."

"Really?" I settled back in the saddle, somewhat reassured.

On and on we rode, as the mountains grew closer and the terrain more rocky. At midmorning we stopped and dismounted, unbridling the horses and tying them to nearby trees. I breathed a sigh of relief—half a morning gone and no incidents from Magic.

The guests were standing around expectantly. I watched Jack build a quick, expert fire with pinyon branches and pine needles as tinder. He nodded at one of the pack mules. "Chloe, can you make some coffee?"

I hurried over to the little mule and unbuckled one of the leather bags strapped to his side. I opened it and extracted a bag of ground coffee and a metal percolator like my grandmother used to have.

The guests distributed themselves on various rocks. The little girls immediately started some kind of complicated game involving several sticks, handfuls of dry aspen leaves, and Miriam's sun hat. I crouched on my heels near the sweet smoky fire and hurriedly scooped grounds into the pot.

Stephen looked over my shoulder. "How much do I put in?" I whispered.

"One scoop," he replied.

"Wrong, brother." Zach had appeared beside us. "Two."

Stephen stiffened immediately. "How the hell do you know?" he replied belligerently.

Zach smiled that supremely confident smile of his. "My grandma had the same coffeepot," he said.

"So?" Stephen scowled at Zach. I felt myself tense up. Rick was eyeing us, waiting for his coffee, no doubt.

"Um, okay, I'll just put in a scoop and a half, okay?" I said in what I hoped was a calm voice.

They subsided, both looking a little abashed, and sat back on their heels. I shoveled the coffee into the pot, and while it bubbled drew Stephen to one side, next to Magic. "Look, you can't let him get under your skin like that," I said to him softly.

He looked at the ground. "I know, but he drives me crazy. I'm just all tense because of my brother. He's been watching these horses. If anything goes wrong, it's on my head."

"What can go wrong?" I asked. "They're doing great." But I felt like I was lying. Magic's fur was warm under my hand, and I leaned against his neck so I wouldn't have to look at Stephen. Rick had said we'd have to cross water this afternoon.

Everyone drank their coffee and mounted up. We continued on the mountain path for a while, then reached a cliff. Rick stopped a safe distance away. He faced us, sweating under the band of his hat.

"Okay," he said. "We're going to go down in the canyon. The path is steep and pretty twisty, so everyone keep a tight hold on your reins and sit back in the saddle."

A little ripple of excitement ran through the line of riders. I felt sick, though. I could see to the bottom of the canyon, as could everyone else. A river coursed through it like a silver line.

Slowly the line of horses started down the steep canyon path. The earth was reddish here, like the Garden of the Gods, and Al's hooves slid in the loose dirt and rocks. I rode carefully, keeping my heels a little forward and down and some slight tension on the reins to help Al balance. In front of me, Magic's haunches swayed back and forth. Mrs. Coleman was doing a decent job riding, I thought. She was straight instead of hunched over the reins, guiding him carefully past the bigger stones in the path. For a long time we swayed down the path without stumbles, until finally it widened out.

We were at the bottom of the small canyon, with the walls standing straight and rocky above us, greenery sprouting from various crevices. Down on the bottom, the dirt was a mix of reddish sand and gravel, with larger boulders lying around, clearly having fallen from the rock walls. We were standing in a wide, flat place, and in front of us a river ran through the canyon, almost without banks. Immediately I could see the change in Magic.

His head was high as he stared at the rushing, burbling water. His ears pricked forward and his nostrils flared. His eyes were wide with apprehension. My own heart beat fast. I looked around. Stephen and Zach were both watching the horse too. For an instant, all of our eyes met.

This is a mistake, I tried to communicate telepathically to them. *He's not ready.* The other horses were already beginning to cross. Rick was at the back, Jack at the front. *Stop, stop!* my mind screamed. But cheerfully, cluelessly, the others were already crossing.

Suddenly, Zach rode up beside me. "He shouldn't cross that river. We have to stop this."

"But how can we?" I hissed. "What would we do? If he can't cross the river, he can't go with the others. Mrs. Coleman won't have a horse to ride—what's she going to do? She'd have to go back, and Rick would have to go with her. He'd be so mad."

Zach's eyes bored into mine. "You and I both know he's not ready." He held my gaze.

"I know," I agreed. "He's not. But Stephen wants him to be." Magic was next in line to cross the river.

"Forget him—that horse should not go near water." Zach wheeled around and quickly trotted back toward Rick.

Magic was balking at the edge. But Mrs. Coleman kept urging him forward, and he kept raising his nose higher and higher to avoid the bit. She didn't realize she was tightening the reins more and more, yet still pressing him forward, unable to understand why he didn't cross.

He was getting more and more agitated. I could see his whole hide quivering. Finally, in exasperation, she gave him a firm kick—as we'd taught her in lessons. He exploded into the air with a massive buck. Everyone gasped. Mrs. Coleman hung on, though she was being thrown about like a rag doll until, with another buck, he pitched her from his back. I gasped as I watched her body make a parabola in the air. She landed with a splash in the river.

Magic, freed of his burden and giving way to his fear, wheeled around with a squeal and galloped away down the canyon, his reins trailing.

In an instant Jack was off his horse and plunging into the river, where Mrs. Coleman was now floating like a bag of old clothes. Sandra clucked to her horse and galloped off down the canyon bed after Magic.

We all held our breath as Jack, waist-deep in the water, towed Mrs. Coleman toward the rocky shore. He and Rick, who had tossed his reins to Stephen, manhandled her onto dry land. No one moved a muscle as Jack, his face frantic, knelt beside her, his ear to her mouth. He laid his hands on her chest and pushed once, twice, the way I'd seen in my Red Cross CPR course. Nothing. She lay still, her head flopped to one side, her mouth open. On one side of her head I could see a deep gash trickling blood. I had a sense of unreality, as if everything before me might be a dream.

No one dared even breathe. The Taylor mother was sobbing quietly. I could hear her gasping behind me, and I wanted to turn and scream in her face. Another push. *Please, please, please,* my mind pleaded over and over. Another.

Mrs. Coleman turned her head. Once, then twice—then she opened her eyes. A gasp and a cheer went up from all of us watching. I felt like I was hearing the blast of trumpets.

"What?" she tried to say, struggling to sit up. "What happened?"

"It's okay." Jack helped her to sit up. "The horse threw you and you landed in the river." He was motioning to Rick. "You're going to be all right, but we have to get you back."

The guests surrounded her, each offering advice. I sought Stephen's eyes, but he turned his face away from me. He was clearly furious. Still, I argued in my mind, Magic wasn't ready—he never should have come. Now a guest had been hurt, and I couldn't help feeling like it had been his fault.

Zach had been right. He'd said the horse wasn't ready and he wasn't. I knew it. We both knew it. I looked at him, but he was dabbing a wet cloth to Mrs. Coleman's head as Rick opened the first aid kit.

Stephen rode up beside me. "What a mess," he said. "That horse screwed up."

I looked at him as if I were seeing him for the first time. "The *horse?*" I said. "The *horse* screwed up? He's afraid of water, Stephen! He never should have come, but you forced him!" I cried.

Stephen gaped at me, but I didn't have the patience to apologize. I turned Al and trotted away.

Mrs. Coleman was transported out by a truck that Sandra had driven in. Magic had been caught a half mile away, heading for home, and put back in the stable. The other guests had decided they wanted to proceed, and we had safely crossed the river and were now bedded down before the campfire that Rick had made. We were camped in a sheltered pine grove on the other side of the canyon. All around us were firs, draping their weeping needles in long bunches to the ground. It was dark, and I lay with my head outside my tent, staring up at the endless sky.

No one knew what would happen now. The trip would go on, but what about the horse? I hadn't spoken to Stephen since my outburst. I felt all snarled up inside. I didn't know what would happen—to Magic, to Stephen, or to me or Zach. After all, we were all supposed to be training the horse, though Stephen was the only one with the high stakes.

Not for the first time, I felt a gulf between me and Stephen. Zach had been right all along. I'd sensed it, but I hadn't acknowledged it—until now. I felt as if a shadow had been lifted from my eyes.

"Psst."

I lifted my head. Zach was leaning over on one elbow. I hadn't realized he was in the neighboring tent. "If you can't sleep, look for the Little Dipper." His eyes were like two deep caverns in the dark shadows of his face.

I raised up on my own elbow. "How do you know I can't sleep?"

He laid back down. "I could just tell."

We were quiet then, but for the rest of the night I could sense him nearby and found myself oddly comforted.

Chapter ✷ Thirteen

The rest of the pack trip continued in a dispirited way. It was a sad climax to the summer, ruined by anxiety over Mrs. Coleman—though we'd heard that she was recovering okay after getting a few stitches—with a general pall cast by the incident. It had rained during the night, and everything was damp and miserable. We visited the waterfall—the big goal of the trip—and viewed it in a cursory manner. Even a small herd of antelope feeding brought no cries of excitement, just a few listless photos snapped.

We trailed back to the ranch early in the afternoon, damp and rumpled, dirt-splotched. The Taylor girls squalled with temper, slapping at each other from their ponies until their father finally turned around and yelled "Stop!" in their faces in such an uncharacteristic display of pique that they immediately fell silent, sniveling. Rick rode in silence, his face set in harsh lines, betraying nothing, while Stephen kept to himself, at the back, away from all of us. He'd barely said a word since the incident.

My own head ached abominably, and I knew I looked terrible—my hair tied up in a bandanna that did little to disguise how greasy it was. My eyes had dark circles under them, I saw this morning in my pocket mirror, and my sinuses felt swollen and ached. Possibly I was allergic to the pine needles.

The guests dismounted in silence and untacked their horses as we'd taught them. Jack led them over to the main house to pep them up with some coffee and to visit Mrs. Coleman.

Rick took Stephen over to a corner by the stable. I couldn't hear what he was saying, but he was leaning in close, his seamed face only a few inches from Stephen's downcast one. Without a word, Zach and I funneled horses into their stalls and handed the saddles over the top to Dana like machines. We curried everyone, brushed and watered everyone, and threw flakes of hay into their hay racks.

"Good trip, guys." Dana tried to speak encouragingly, and I gave her a dutiful smile. She patted me on the back and started lugging saddles to the tack room.

I picked up a water bucket to scrub it, but set it down and sighed. I had to talk to Magic. I walked down to his stall and we faced each other. "Hey, buddy," I said softly, and leaned against his neck, putting my arms around him and inhaling his horsey, wet-sweater-leather-and-hay scent. I stayed that way for a long time, just standing there with him, feeling the heat radiating from his good, solid flesh. "What's going to happen to you?" I whispered.

He couldn't tell me, of course. That's when I felt a hand on my back. I looked up and there was Zach. "I'm sorry, Chloe."

Something was odd about the sentence—then I realized it was the first time I'd ever heard him use my first name.

"Let's get out of here," he said suddenly.

I looked up, startled. "What?"

"Come on." A glint came into his face. "I'm breaking you out." Without another word he took my hand and ran me out of the stable toward the pickups parked in front of the main house.

"Where are we going?" I panted behind him.

"Anywhere but here!" he called over his shoulder. He ran from truck to truck, looking inside each window. I realized he was looking for keys, and he must have found one with them because he called, "Come on, get in!"

Breathless, wondering if we were going to get arrested for something like this, I slid across the bench seat as he slammed the truck door and fired up the engine with a deafening roar. It sounded like the muffler was missing. "Where are we going? What are you doing?" I yelled over the noise of the engine as he roared down the driveway in a cloud of dust. "Are you stealing this car? Zach? Do you mind telling me what the hell's going on?"

"Don't worry!" he shouted. The windows of the truck seemed to be permanently stuck in the down position, and the wind blew through the cab, taking our words and throwing them back outside. I spit my hair out of my face where it whipped wildly, like a scarf in the breeze. "We're just going on a little adventure!"

"An adventure that's going to land us in jail!" I shouted back, suddenly exhilarated by the speed and the rocking of the truck. All I'd done was worry these last few days, and I wanted to stop. I wanted to forget everything—and find the adventure I'd come out here for.

"We need to get away," Zach said, as if reading my thoughts. "That place is depressing—it was bringing me down. Let's go have some fun."

"Wait, wait, stop!" I shouted suddenly. He screeched the brakes. "Tacos!"

There beside the road was a building that looked like it had once been a garage but was now painted hot pink. Cactuses and tubs of desert flowers were scattered around. The door was rolled up, revealing a counter and a few tables scattered around. LA CASITA was painted in purple on the handmade sign out front.

"I'm starving!" I declared, and leaped from the car. I felt like a different person—it was as if Zach's crazy spirit had infected me.

We raced up to the counter and scanned the brief menu. "Two beef tacos," Zach said, "and two orange pops."

"Absolutely, sir," said a small, dark-haired girl in a rock band T-shirt. She punched in our order and three minutes later handed us the warm tacos, bundled in paper like two little animals, and two bottles of ice-cold, bright orange pop.

We carried our food outside and sat on the top of a picnic

table, our feet dangling, our shoulders almost touching as we crunched the crispy corn tacos and the soft, hot beef inside.

"Oh my God, this is incredible," I sighed, swigging from my bottle of pop. "You have no idea how down I was getting after the Magic incident."

For an instant Zach looked angry again. "I can't believe he—" He stopped himself. For a moment he was quiet, looking across the parking lot. Then his eyes lit up and he jumped off the bench, grabbing my hand again. "Come on! I know the perfect adventure place!"

We got back into the truck and roared off, trailing blue exhaust. "Isn't Jack going to wonder where his truck is?" I asked.

Zach looked almost guilty for a minute, then confessed. "Actually, he told me I could have the afternoon off and you too, and that I could take a truck. He knew we needed a break. I just wanted you to think I was taking it without permission."

I laughed. "Oh, so you're not such a bad boy after all!" I teased. "Here I thought you were stealing a truck and you were actually just following orders, is that it?"

He turned onto a small road and then another, the asphalt disappearing to dirt. The mountains were close now, and the truck climbed a steep, twisty road. A drop on the right side disappeared into a dense pine forest. The sun shot shafts of light through the trees, making the scene look like something from the children's Bible I had growing up. I leaned out the window, just catching sight of a large buck slipping between the trees.

At the top of a foothill, Zach pulled over and killed the engine. In the loud silence I opened the door and got out. We were in the middle of the pine forest, hills all around us, not a soul in sight.

"Is this the adventure?" I asked, puzzled.

"The adventure's around here somewhere," he said. "I just have to remember where the path starts—ah! There it is!" He pointed to a small dirt road leading down into the forest a short distance from where he'd parked the truck. I looked down the hill, then back at Zach.

"That's an adventure?" I teased. "Looks thrilling."

A smile quirked the corners of his mouth. "Just you wait. It's at the bottom." He paused. "Which I will get to first." He took off down the hill.

"No, you won't!" I screeched, stumbling after him, my heels sliding in the dirt, clutching trees and small bushes. Laughing, I reached out and just managed to snag the back of his T-shirt, pulling him backward and throwing him off balance enough that he tumbled into the spiny scrub at the side of the path.

"Hey now!" He rolled over and looked up at me from his absurd position, lying among the sagebrush, a smear of dirt across his forehead. "You're in trouble now, you know."

"Oh yeah? Actually, it looks like *you're* in trouble."

He reached up and, before I could even react, pulled me down beside him. With that one movement I sensed we'd crossed an invisible line we'd only been circling before. I knew Zach sensed it too. I didn't know what would happen, though. I didn't want to try to figure it out. Instead I squirmed around in my bed of crushed sagebrush until I could see the sky. The aroma of the sage was strong in the afternoon sun.

We lay there in silence for a while, staring up. The sky seemed to go on forever and ever. I thought of the vastness of it, the blue fading to black and then the cold brilliance of space, with all the stars going on and on and back forever. I shook my head and raised up on my elbows. I was making myself dizzy.

I looked over at Zach, who was lying on his back, his eyes closed. His black hair was damp at his temples. "Zach. You know, Stephen and I—"

He sat up suddenly and plucked a few leaves from beside him. "Smell this."

"Zach—"

"Come on."

Clearly, he didn't want to hear what I had to say about Stephen. I reached out to take the leaves, but he grasped my hand instead, his fingers wrapping powerfully around my wrist. He looked right into my face, and I felt my whole body grow hot. He turned my hand palm up and then slowly rubbed the crushed sage leaves across the skin of my wrist. "There." He released my hand.

My mouth was dry, I noticed, and I could feel the imprint of his fingers as if they were branded onto my hand. I sniffed the sharp, spicy aroma.

He smiled down at me, and then we struggled up from the sage and started back along the path again. At the bottom of the hill, he stopped. "This is it—at least, I think. It looks a little different."

I looked around. We were standing on the overgrown edge of a tiny dirt road. Right next to the road and down a steep bank, a mountain river flowed, the dark water sparkling as it foamed over the rocks in its midst. On the opposite side, an aspen wood spread its cool greenness as far as I could see. There was no one around.

"Come on!" Zach grabbed my hand excitedly, and we scrambled down the bank. I saw a small trail weaving its way among the rocks at the river's edge. Zach led me along it as the river meandered away from the road.

In twenty minutes we were in another rocky, piney woods, with the rushing, icy-cold river providing the background to the liquid trills of the blackbirds. The air was damp from the cold water, and everywhere crashed-over pine trees were layered with soft moss in every shade of green, from deepest green-black to shocking lime green. I paused and, laying my cheek down on the edge of a big log, looked sideways at the moss. I was at eye level with the tiny plant, and from this view, what looked like fuzzy velvet from above I could see was a lot of tiny, springy plants, each distinct, like a forest for the tiniest fairies.

Suddenly I heard a screech from above, and Zach grabbed my arm, pointing up. I gasped as I saw a flash of dark wings and then the unmistakable white head and curled yellow claws of a bald eagle. We watched, frozen with awe, as the huge bird, bigger than

I'd ever imagined, climbed higher and higher into the azure sky until it remained there, soaring on an invisible plume of air, the black wings still distinct even hundreds of feet up.

Panting, we scrambled over the tree trunks with huge, knotty roots that grew almost to the river's edge, climbing over gray boulders scattered like a giant's playthings. Then Zach pointed. "There! I can't believe it's still there." He stood perfectly still. I came up beside him, my breathing suddenly loud in the silence.

He stood still for what seemed like a long time, then spoke. "We came here, when I was a kid, you know. My brother and me." His voice caught on the last sentence.

I stayed quiet, but my mind flashed to the creased photo I'd picked up in the tack room. Zach didn't look at me, just slowly walked over to a cluster of gray stones arranged in the river, at the very edge by the bank. "We'd come every time we came to Colorado—we never knew if the springs would still be here, or if the rocks had been washed away by floods, or if someone else had found it and built a path and handrails, or if there'd be a big sign telling us not to swim."

He walked up to the rocks, squatted down on his heels, and dabbled his fingers in the water. I moved beside him and waited. "There was always this big anticipation whenever we'd come around this corner. One year there were a bunch of college kids here. They were cool, though—they offered Dan and me beer even though I was like nine. My parents thought that was hilarious." He smiled an inward smile. "Another time, Dan was goofing around in the river, pretending like he was drowning, going 'help, help.' And this guy was here with his huge German shepherd, and the dog jumps in the river and swims over and takes Dan's arm, but really gently, and starts *towing* him to the edge, then trying to drag him out onto the bank." He shook his head. "We talked about that for years. What a cool dog."

He dabbled his fingers in the water some more, then looked up in my direction, though I could tell he wasn't really looking at me. "Then he went off on this trip to the Tetons. He'd gotten all into rock climbing since getting to college. He had all the ropes, the shoes, and everything. It was cool, he—" His voice thickened and caught. He fought against himself, then went on. "He was going to take me to Kentucky when he got back. We were going to go together." A tear slid down his cheek. "Then the guy he was going to the Tetons with canceled at the last minute, and my dad convinced him to do what was right and not take any of his ropes if he was going by himself. He wouldn't have anyone to belay; it wouldn't be *safe*." He swallowed hard. I saw the cords standing out on the side of his neck. "He didn't—he said he wouldn't do any technical climbing, just scrambling. But he was an idiot, he screwed it up and went off the path, behind the signs that said it was unsafe, too steep. He fell. He fell three hundred feet. And it was two days before a ranger found him."

He went silent, staring straight ahead. I stayed quiet by his side. Finally I tentatively touched his back. "Zach, that's so awful." I wanted to cry myself, his story was so sad.

"My mom fell to the ground when she heard. She just fell over and curled up. I slept in his bed that night. I couldn't think of any other way to be close to him."

He fell silent, but I sensed there was something he was holding back.

I leaned forward and placed my hand on his knee. "What?"

"It's just that this photo—I had this picture of Dan and me. It's from a few weeks before he died. When I knew I was going to come out here for the summer, and the springs were so close, I brought it with me. I wanted to leave it out here, to remember him. But I lost it. I don't know where. Probably slipped out of my pocket when I was working."

"Zach—" Then I stopped. Something held me back. I didn't tell him I'd found it on the feed room floor. It felt too intimate, somehow—like I'd peeped into a curtained window. "Are you sad you came back here?" I asked instead.

He considered and shook his head.

"No, I'm happy, actually. I like thinking of all of us here. I'm glad it's still here—Dan would've liked that."

"And that night, in the common room?"

"Oh. That." He cleared his throat and traced a circle on the log. "We went out to get his truck, all the way out to the Tetons, to get it from the trailhead where he'd left it." He wiped the corner of his mouth with a thumb. "That song was on the CD player when we turned the car on. He'd been listening to a John Denver mix I'd made for him before he left."

My own throat swelled and ached, and I struggled not to cry. Zach saw my face, though, and reached out and took my hand. We sat together on the log for a long time, not speaking, our fingers clasped together.

Then Zach looked around himself like he was coming out of a dream, and some of the hot mischievousness came back into his eyes. "Anyway, let's go in." He stood up and pulled off his shirt, then dipped a foot in the water. The muscles in his smooth back rippled under his skin. He climbed down over the rocks and yelled. "Owee, that's hot!" The steam was rising up all around him. At least I'd worn a sports bra under my tank top today, and some pretty tight running shorts. I stripped off my shirt, sort of hoping Zach would be looking and sort of hoping he wouldn't.

And Zach didn't look away or anything modest and helpful, like Stephen would have. He grinned, as if he knew exactly what I was thinking, his ice-blue eyes twinkling until my face was flaming.

"Well, don't you want to test the water?" I finally said, mostly because I felt like I was going to burst into flames if I stood there one more minute with his smoldering gaze looking me up and down. I turned my back on him and, resting my hands on the slippery gray rocks, lowered myself partly into the water.

I gasped involuntarily. "It's really hot!" It was a surreal sensation, the hot water surrounding me as I gazed out at the ferns and slick, moss-covered rocks, and beyond them the pine trees dripping long green needles, and beyond them the blue mountains, looking like a picture you might find hanging over your bed in a cheap hotel—too clichéd to be real. Except they were.

A strong scent rose up in the steam. "Am I smelling rotten eggs?" I looked over at Zach, who had gotten into the pool and was standing waist-deep beside me.

He grinned and inhaled deeply. "Mmm, my favorite!"

I wrinkled my nose. "Ew, seriously?"

"It's the sulfur from the spring—that's what makes it smell that way. It's supposed to be good for you."

I inhaled again. It didn't seem so bad now, mixed with the fresh, earthy scents of the forest around us.

Gingerly, I felt my way through the murky water. The bottom was small rocks and sandy mud. I wondered if there were fish or other animals that I might step on. Something brushed my leg, and I shrieked and grabbed at Zach's arm before I realized it was the edge of Zach's shorts.

The water was hotter near the bottom, where it burbled out from the depths of the earth, and cooler on the top. It was a natural spring that existed to the side of the river, but clearly, over the years people had created the pool by stacking up large and small stones to capture the hot water and protect it from the snow-cold river. I felt my way across the bottom, trying not to stumble, and perched on a big rock under the water.

"Zach, this is seriously incredible." I felt like I was calming down after our crazy ride through the forest. I leaned back on the rocks and spread my arms out, starting up at the insanely blue sky.

It seemed very weird to be looking up at trees and feeling rocks under my arms, smelling that dank sulfur smell, instead of the scent of chlorine and feeling concrete around me like when I was in a swimming pool. "This is so warm!"

He grinned and splashed me and I shrieked and splashed him back, the hot water making a delicious contrast with the droplets of ice cold spraying from the river immediately beside us. "Here, come on!" Zach scrambled over the rocks separating the spring pool from the river. "Yeoow!" he yelled as he plunged into the icy-cold water.

"Are you crazy?" I shouted at him, huddling lower in the hot spring pool. "I always knew you were nuts!"

He swam up to the pool, smiling diabolically. "And you're going in with me!" He reached over the rocks and grabbed my upper arm.

"No!" I shrieked, trying to swim away. But he was too strong and hauled me over the slippery rocks.

I screamed as I plunged into the rushing river, clutching Zach around the neck. He wrapped his arms around me, laughing, and pressed me close against him under the water.

For an instant our bare legs swam deliciously together, and I could feel his chest and belly against mine. Then I pulled away, overwhelmed suddenly by the feeling of his bare skin, and swam a few feet off to hide my confusion and my red cheeks. He must have felt the same way, because he didn't say anything, but just swam in a circle.

"Look up there." He pointed at the mountains on the horizon. Fluffy white clouds sat on the mountaintops like heaped-up pillows. They looked innocuous enough.

"Yeah? They're called clouds—have you ever seen them before?" I teased.

Thunder cracked overhead, startling me, and I looked up, my feet fumbling for purchase on the slippery rocks of the river bottom. Dark-gray clouds had rolled in fast and were churning in the sky.

Zach swam over. "Come on, we've got to get under something quick—these mountain storms can be wicked in the summer, especially at this altitude." His eyes were sparkling, though, his wet hair pasted to his forehead in black spikes. I knew he was loving the danger, in spite of his cautious words.

Thunder boomed again and lightning flashed. The sound echoed off the mountains. The wind picked up. "Come on!" Zach started swimming toward the bank, shoving me in front of him. We scrambled up the rocks, out of the water, just as the rain started. The drops pelted us with ferocious intensity.

"Ow!" I cried as the little drops hit my bare back. They felt as hard as BBs. The aspen leaves rustled around us as the drops fell with the patter of a million tiny feet. Thunder cracked, and then something exploded next to us and a white flash blinded me. The air was full of electric prickles. I screamed and clutched Zach, burying my head in his chest. "What was that?" I gasped.

"Lightning struck that tree!" he shouted over the thunder.

He pointed to the smoldering remains of a giant pine tree, now split almost in half, burned black and smoking. We ran along the bank, looking for somewhere, anywhere to shelter. Then the rain changed—hard rocks were hitting my back and shoulders. "Hail, Zach!" I yelled. The hailstones were getting larger and larger. They were the size of gumballs now. "Ow! Ow!"

We scrambled back down the bank, closer to the river again, the hailstones leaving red welts on our skin everywhere they hit. "Zach!" I was panicky now, trying to cover my head with my hands. "Zach!"

"Here! Get under here!" He pulled me roughly under a shelf of projecting rock sticking out from the bank. Crouching down, we could both just fit underneath, with the river rushing just a few feet below.

Somewhat sheltered, I huddled close to Zach, trying to catch my breath. "Oh my God!" I squeaked.

He was breathing hard too, but his blue eyes had lost none of their merriment. "Don't worry, we're not going to die," he teased, his breath warm on my cheek.

"I know that!" I replied, automatically indignant. I realized that our faces were just inches apart. My breath suddenly stopped and I looked into his eyes. He held my gaze and then his eyes dropped to my lips. My heart gave a great thud. "Zach . . . ," I whispered.

He touched my wet hair where it lay over my shoulder. "What?"

"I . . ." But I didn't know what I was going to say. I only knew how my body felt at this moment—like I wanted nothing more in the world but to press my lips against his.

He leaned in a little, and just then, dirt and rocks slid out from beneath his feet and he tumbled down the bank, splashing into the river.

"Zach!" I screamed in momentary panic, but the water was only a few feet deep, I saw, and he was already scrambling to his feet.

The rain was letting up too, and the hail slowed and then stopped, as quickly as it had begun. I eased out from under the rock as Zach climbed back up the bank.

"*That* was quick." I gave a little laugh and tried to brush some of the mud and leaves off my arms and legs, suddenly self-conscious.

"Yeah. That was intense." Zach was giving a scratch on his arm a long inspection. I wondered if he felt a little embarrassed, the way he'd opened up to me.

"I've been thinking about a problem," I said slowly.

"Really?"

"You seem surprised." I sat down on one of the big rocks.

"It's just that you seem like the type never to have problems."

"That's cute, but I do have a problem." I traced a pine needle on the rock so I wouldn't have to look at him.

"What is it?"

"Well . . ." I swallowed. "There's these two guys. And I thought I liked one. But now . . . I'm not so sure."

Zach's brow was knitted quizzically. "Wait a minute. . . ."

I held up my hand. "Hang on. I'm not done. The one guy seemed perfect at first. And he still kind of is. It's just there's this other guy—kind of annoying. Kind of cocky. But I can't stay away from him. . . ." I finally raised my eyes to his.

He was grinning. "The second guy sounds like kind of a jerk. Not the type for a nice girl like you."

"I know! I should probably run away, right?" Now my smile matched his. My cheeks ached with it, but I didn't care.

Zach reached out and touched a wet strand of my hair where it lay over my shoulder. "Only you know what's best for you. You have to do what you feel like you have to do." He clasped my hand in his, intertwining our fingers.

"I know what's best," I said softly. "It's right here in front of me."

Chapter ● Fourteen

Muddy and tired, we pulled up to the main house with the sun low in the sky, shooting long golden rays across the pastures. I felt drained but in a good way. The day seemed like it had been the longest day—the longest two days—ever. Zach took my hand briefly as we got down from the truck and I let him. My mind was all mixed up. I didn't know what was happening with him, with Stephen, but I did know that I felt good—really good. I smiled at him. "I just want to say good night to Magic before dinner," I said.

"I'll come with you." We hurried toward the stable and ran down the aisle. I stopped short. Magic's stall door was open, sawdust trailing from the entrance. Magic was gone.

"What? Where is he?" I looked around wildly.

"Don't worry," Zach reassured me. "They probably just turned him out early." The other horses were still in their stalls.

"Oh, right." I felt silly for reacting so strongly. We walked out toward the pasture, and then I froze just outside the opposite stable door. A truck was pulled up there, with a trailer attached. Magic was in the trailer, the door shut and locked. "What's going on?" I gasped.

I heard voices from around the side of the truck and stepped around. Stephen was standing there, talking on a two-way radio. "What's going on?" I asked him, trying to stay calm. "Is he hurt?" Maybe he was just taking Magic to the vet.

Stephen lowered the radio. "He's leaving." He wouldn't look at either of us.

"What do you mean, leaving?" Zach asked. I could tell he was trying to keep a hold of his temper, but I knew him well enough now to know it wouldn't last long.

"I mean Rick wants him to go back. We're driving him to the market now—there's a big auction tomorrow." He spoke to the truck door.

"What!" My heart was hammering. "What are you talking about? You're sending him away? Our Magic?"

"He's not safe! He screwed up and hurt a guest!" Stephen's voice rose.

My own temper tore loose. "He screwed up because you pushed him!" I screamed back, almost in his face. "You knew, you knew he was afraid of water and you made him go on the trip and across that river because all the horses had to be ready!"

"Rick's pissed, okay?" Stephen said. "I told him I'd take care of the situation, and this is how it's happening."

"So you're hiding the evidence, is that right?" Zach broke in. His voice was full of barely restrained fury.

"That's not how it is!" Stephen yelled. His voice broke. Shockingly, I heard tears behind the anger. "Look, this horse screwed up all my chances, do you get it? This was supposed to be my summer—it *would've* been my summer, if it weren't for him!"

We were quiet, shocked into silence by his painfully screwed-up face. Behind him, Magic looked placidly over the edge of the half door of the trailer. He didn't know he was going to be sold.

I couldn't bear the trusting look on his calm face any longer. I walked up the still-lowered trailer ramp and slid back the metal latch.

"What are you doing?" Stephen said.

Calmly, I fastened the lead rope to the horse's halter and pushed open the door. "I'm putting him back in his stall," I said, shocked at my own boldness. "He's not going anywhere tonight. If Rick has a problem with that, I'll tell him it was my decision."

They were silent behind me as I led the horse down the ramp.

But later that evening my resolve left me. Zach found me seated at the table in the empty common room, my head in my hands. The sobs poured out of me. I felt a hand on my back and looked up briefly. Zach was standing beside me. After a minute he sat down in the seat next to me and rubbed my shoulders. My sobs emptied themselves out.

I sat up and wiped my nose on my sleeve, not caring how gross it was. "He tried," I said thickly. "He worked so hard. *We* worked so hard. Just to have that jerked away because of one stupid mistake? It's unbearable how unfair it is." I dropped my head in my hands and felt the hot tears drop from my eyes. "And you know the worst part?"

Zach held out a tissue and I took it. "The worst part," I choked out, "is how scared he's going to be. He's going to think I just left him—right after he finally learned to trust me." The sobs overwhelmed me again as I thought of the uncomprehending animal's fear and confusion. I pictured him standing on the platform at the auction market, a chalked number on his side, trembling at the strange noises and rough hands grabbing him, examining his teeth.

Zach rested his hand on my back and said nothing. He didn't have to. I knew he felt as awful as I did.

Then he stood up. I looked up at him through tear-bleared eyes. "What are you doing?" I asked.

"Come on." He turned around. "We're not giving up."

I followed him automatically, though I still didn't know what he was talking about. "Giving up what?"

"Giving up on that horse," he said, and strode determinedly from the room.

I followed him out into the deep mountain night. The air was cool and dry, scented with pine, and the familiar ranch looked eerie under the strong moonlight pouring down. "Zach, what are you doing?"

He didn't answer, just grabbed my hand firmly in his and walked toward the stable.

Inside, the horses were quiet, sleeping, their heads turned toward the backs of their stalls. Here and there I heard the shifting of a body or the clink of a water bucket against the wall. Zach led me toward Magic's stall in the middle. "Hey boy," he whispered. "Wake up!"

Magic turned from the back of the stall to face us. I imagined that his large eyes were questioning. Zach slid back the bolt and held out a lead rope, which I clipped onto the halter. I had an idea now of where we were headed, and my excitement rose as Magic stepped willingly from the stall.

Together we stole across the moonlit field like two thieves in the night, our precious booty walking behind us, his hooves thunking the ground rhythmically, comfortingly. On and on we walked, one on either side of the horse's head, until we came to the stream where Stephen had forced Magic across that day.

We stopped him a short distance from the water, and there I patted him and Zach talked to him. We spent a long time fussing over him, and then I took his big head in both of my hands and looked him deep in the eyes. "Magic," I said seriously. He looked back at me as if he could understand me perfectly. "We know you can do this. You've been doing great." I didn't want to remind him of the Mrs. Coleman incident. "You've been doing great," I repeated. "Now we're just going to practice a little more." I didn't want to tell him this was his last chance. No sense in laying on the pressure if it wasn't necessary.

Zach took a small can out of his pocket and shook it. Magic and I looked around. Sweet feed, the sticky, molasses-coated grain no horse could resist. Magic's ears pricked. I dipped my hand into the can and let him lick up a small mouthful from my hand.

Then, talking to him soothingly all the while, I led him across the tussocky grass a little closer to the stream, which was trickling blackly among the grasses. He came willingly, though I sensed the tension increasing in his body. "Here, boy," I said cheerfully, making sure my body never betrayed the gravity of the situation. Quietly, Zach tipped a handful of the grain from the can, then nodded at me and splashed across the small creek to the other side.

I led Magic closer to the stream and, when I sensed his hesitation, palmed a few grains of sweet feed between his lips. At the banks of the stream he hesitated. Immediately, Zach rattled the can enticingly. The horse's ears pricked up, and before he had a chance to think, I quickened my step. "Come on, boy!" I cried, and before he realized what was happening, he had splashed across the stream, led by my rope. The second he reached the other side, Zach held out a huge handful of grain, which he eagerly slurped up.

Zach and I looked at each other in delight and triumph. "He did it!" I cried joyfully.

"Thanks to you," Zach said. I flung my arms around his

neck without thinking. Our faces were very close, and for a long moment we looked at each other. Then slowly, without hurrying, he placed his hands on either side of my face and drew me to him. He tilted his head and pressed his lips softly, slowly to mine. The kiss seemed to go on forever, though I know it was only a few seconds. But in that instant, the whole world narrowed down to the sensation of his hot mouth on mine, pressing firmly and insistently, the feel of his hands buried in my hair, caressing my neck, just as I'd always dreamed.

He raised his head and we looked at each other. "Zach," I breathed. He held his finger to my lips.

"Don't say anything."

Magic crossed the stream six more times that night.

When we finally walked back to the stable, Magic clopping along placidly behind us, snorting his warm breath, I felt Zach's hand reach out and entwine with mine. I didn't know what to think, but then again, nothing this summer had turned out like I'd expected. All I knew was what was happening now—Zach had kissed me and Magic had crossed the water. I had no expectations anymore, because I could no longer predict what would happen.

Chapter ✤ Fifteen

The next morning Zach, Magic, and I crossed the pasture again. This time, the sun shone down brightly on our heads, and there were two more people with us: At breakfast I had, as politely as I could, asked Rick and Stephen to come down to the stream.

Rick looked grumpy, but at least he was coming with us. Stephen wouldn't look at anyone. He just stared down at the grass as he walked. Magic was scheduled to go out to the auction in one hour.

My stomach was in knots. I didn't know where to look—at Stephen, who I felt I'd betrayed somehow by kissing Zach last night; at Zach, who I could hardly look at after our romantic moment; or at Rick, who I was terrified would still send Magic away, even if he could cross the stream.

We reached the banks of the stream and stopped. "Well?"

Rick barked. "I've got a lot to do, folks, and this horse is scheduled to go to the auction mart in one hour. The rest of the horses need to be turned out, Stephen and Zach."

"I know," Zach said, holding up his hand. "This will only take a minute, and it's important."

"He deserves another chance," I said, trying to keep the emotion out of my voice. "We practiced with him last night." I nodded to Zach, and we took our positions, one on either side of the creek, with the sweet feed at the ready. Once again I patted Magic and spoke to him. I could sense his willingness and his trust in me. Once again I gave him a handful of grain, and then another. Zach shook the can. Immediately, before he had time to get nervous, I led him swiftly and calmly across the stream, his hooves splashing and the water flying up to wet his belly. Zach gave him a handful of grain on the other side, and there he stood, chewing it as if he'd never been afraid of water in his life.

"Well, I'll be," Rick said, and spit into the creek. "I never thought that horse would cross water. Not after what happened."

Zach and I looked at each other in triumph. Had we done it? I looked at Stephen.

He wouldn't meet my eyes.

"That's something," Rick said again. This was the most I'd heard him talk all summer. I guess it took a horse to really get him going.

"I think he just needs a little more work," I said, and held my breath. Rick was the ultimate decider, so this was it.

"Maybe . . ." He tapped his teeth with his forefinger and then nodded. "Maybe. I'll talk to Jack." He strode off abruptly, then stopped and fixed Stephen with a look. "We'll talk later."

For a moment our little group around the creek just stood there awkwardly. Zach touched my shoulder, then dropped his hand quickly. He looked from me to Stephen and then back again.

"Well!" he said. "I think I'll just take Magic back." With uncharacteristic tact, he quickly took the lead rope out of my hands and led Magic away toward the stable.

Stephen and I looked at each other. Finally, I broke the silence. "Well," I said.

"Well."

Then we were quiet again.

"I guess you and I are over," Stephen said.

I looked at him quickly to detect any bitterness. But there was only sad resignation in his face.

"I guess I blew it, huh?" he said.

I reached out, but he took a step back. "You didn't blow it. It just wasn't meant to be." I paused. "Believe me, I never thought it would turn out this way either." I suppressed a smile, and he started grinning too.

"Me neither," he said. "He's kind of cocky."

"I used to think that too," I said.

Then he dropped the jocular smile. "I guess I'm not really ready to talk about it."

"That's okay. I understand."

We started back across the grass together. "What's going to happen to you?" I felt like I could say anything to him now. There were no more secrets.

He shrugged. "I don't know. Talk to my brother, I guess. I think my chances for a promotion are shot."

I thought so too. But probably saying so wouldn't help. "Nothing about this summer has turned out the way I thought it would."

"Me neither, honestly." He was quiet again. He seemed to be thinking about something.

At the door of the stable, Zach was clustered with Dana, both of them talking quietly. They broke off when we came up. Stephen faced Zach. "Look, I couldn't stand you most of this summer and I'm not sure I can now, but when I'm wrong, I say I'm wrong. And I was." He stuffed his hands in his pockets and stared past Zach's shoulder at a clump of unwashed halters hanging on the wall.

Dana stepped on my foot and, when I looked at her, jerked her head slightly to the side. I got her point. Discreetly, we strolled a few steps away. Not so far that we couldn't hear, though.

"Okay, that's cool," Zach replied. "Look, it's in the past, okay? Let's just forget about it."

"No, it's not." Stephen scowled at the halters. "I'm pissed off at myself. It was just like I got tunnel vision at the end. And now I've screwed it up." He looked down the row of stalls at the horses hanging their heads out. As if listening, Magic turned and gazed at him with his big, bright eyes.

A thought was sizzling around in my mind. I turned suddenly and ran out of the stable.

"Hey, where're you going?" Dana called.

"Just to see Rick and Jack," I called back.

I found them talking seriously in the office, behind the desk of heaped-up papers. I didn't need a degree in rocket science to figure out that Rick was filling Jack in on the Magic situation. They broke off their conversation when they heard my footsteps and turned to me in the doorway.

Jack looked over a stack of file folders. "What's going on, Chloe? Aside from your presentation in the pasture this morning. Rick's been telling me about it. Not totally according to the rules, as I'm sure you know."

I flushed and looked down at my boots. They were even more creased and dusty than when Dana had given them to me at the beginning of the summer. I wondered what my parents would say when I came home early, without a paycheck, having been kicked out of my summer job.

"Still, nice work," Jack went on. My head jerked up. There was a hint of a smile around his eyes. "I like to see that dedication to the horses. Shows character." He offered me a pawlike hand.

I shook it. "Thanks." I figured I should take my chance, since it looked like I wasn't getting fired after all. "Jack, um, I was wondering—could we take Magic and a couple horses out for a trail ride? The guests are in town, so we wouldn't be interfering with anything. To celebrate Magic's staying and all?"

"Rick, what do you think?" Jack asked. Rick was still standing in the corner, stone-faced, his mustache as bristly and unyielding as ever.

"I don't know that that horse needs any more work."

My stomach sank.

"But I guess an hour wouldn't matter."

I resisted the urge to clap my hands together and instead murmured, "Thanks. We'll just go through the back pastures, past the creek."

"Be sure to clean those bridles when you're done."

"We will," I promised, backing out of the room.

In the sunshine I flew over the grass. The group was clustered together by Magic's stall when I burst into the stable. "Hey, we're going for a trail ride!"

"What?" Dana asked. "Right now?"

I nodded, trying to catch my breath. "All of us. Jack wants Stephen to ride Magic." A little white lie, to get him up on the horse.

"Seriously?" Stephen asked. "Why? What did he say?"

I widened my eyes disingenuously. "That was it! Just that he wanted you to ride Magic."

Dana was watching me closely, and she must have sensed what I was up to, because she sprang into action with Dana-esque efficiency. "Okay, cool! I was dying to ride this morning. I'll take Little Sal. Zach, how about you take Billy, and Chloe can ride Al, okay?"

"What are you doing?" Zach hissed to me as we tacked up.

"Just trust me," I told him.

Almost before we knew what was happening, we were mounted. We were all watching Stephen on Magic, though we were trying not to. He was handling the reins like they were silk. Magic's head was up and he was alert, as if he could tell who was mounted on him. But Stephen moved carefully, very carefully, and when we started out down the path that ran to one side of the pasture, Magic's head relaxed and I let out a huge breath I hadn't even realized I'd been holding. I saw Stephen relax too. His legs lengthened and his hands buried themselves deep in Magic's mane. By the time we trotted to the bottom of the pasture, Stephen was almost smiling.

"So that's what you were up to," Zach said from behind me. "You wanted them to make up."

I twisted around in the saddle. "It didn't seem right to just leave this hanging. Even if we're not getting fired."

Ahead of us, Stephen leaned forward and gave Magic's neck a firm pat. "Good boy," I heard him say.

"All right, guys, let's lope!" Dana shouted back to us. I pressed my heels to Al's sides, and the wind lifted my sweaty hair as we picked up speed. I leaned forward and cantered up beside Magic. On my other side, Zach came even with me, and Dana dropped back until the four of us were riding together over the waving grass, side by side, toward the mountains.

Chapter ● Sixteen

When we finally pushed our way through the last layer of ferns near the hot springs, the sun was setting in flaming curtains of gold and crimson and deep violet. Back at the ranch, my khaki duffel was sitting by the door, neatly zipped. The bureau top was bare of its usual clutter. My flight was at ten o'clock the next morning, the rest of the hands' soon after.

Behind me, Zach leaped lightly over a boulder in our path. "Okay, McKinley, you want to tell me what we're doing again? We already went swimming. But if you're interested in skinny-dipping, then . . ." He reached for me, and I laughed and ran the last few steps to the spring, just out of his reach.

"No, I'm not thinking of that." I swatted his hand away. "Be serious. Here, sit there." I pointed to the log we'd sat on before.

"I love it when you order me around." He grinned.

The hot pool was higher today, and the forest looked different, deeper and more mysterious in the waning light. The steam rising from the water was lit by the sun's long shooting rays, making it look more like a fairyland than ever. "Zach . . . that day in the feed room."

He looked puzzled.

"The day of the hayride," I prompted him. "You were thinking about Dan . . . even though I didn't know that then."

"Oh yeah." His cheeks grew slightly pink.

"Well, I found something that day." I put my hand in my jeans pocket and drew out the battered photo I'd picked up from the floor. I held it toward him.

He leaned forward and took it. "The picture! You had it?" He unfolded it and smoothed out the creases.

I perched next to him. "Yeah. I'm sorry I kept it. But that's why I told you I wanted to come out here again."

Zach looked up, nodding slowly. "Now I can leave it, like I wanted."

I stood up and took his hand, tugging him up from the log. "And say good-bye to Dan."

The soft bubbling of the spring in our ears and the sun dipping lower, we made our way to the edge of the river. Zach knelt down amid the small rocks and feathery ferns crowding the banks. He paused, holding the photo delicately. "This is for you, bro," he said softly, and leaned far out over the water, letting the picture drift from his fingers.

Zach put his arm around me and I laid my head on his shoulder as we watched the small white square swirl away from us, so bright against the dark water, until it disappeared.

"This wasn't exactly what I pictured when I saw you at the airport that first day," I said finally, breaking the silence.

"Oh, right. Private McKinley." He touched my eyebrow gently. "How *is* your eye?"

I smiled. "Just a little scar. Enough to remind me of you."

"What makes you think you'll need reminding?"

"Well, we're leaving. You back to Charleston, me back to Cincinnati." I traced my initials on the knee of his jeans. We rose and wandered back down the path, holding hands.

I looked back at the shadowy spring bubbling quietly behind us, and ahead at the path curving upward, revealing the soft gray-and-rose sky.

"That still doesn't mean I'll need reminding." Zach took both my hands in his and rubbed his thumbs over the backs. "Reminding would mean that somehow I'd forgotten you."

He pulled me toward him and I laid my head on his chest, and we stood together in the forest as the shadows fell around us.

A. DESTINY is the coauthor of the Flirt series. She spends her time reading books, writing, and watching sweet romance movies. She will always remember her first kiss.

EMMA CARLSON BERNE is the author of *Never Let You Go*, *Still Waters*, and *Hard to Get*. She is also the author of *Choker*, under the pseudonym Elizabeth Woods. She lives in Ohio with her family.

TURN THE PAGE FOR MORE FLIRTY FUN.

couldn't quite get the color of her hair right.

I stepped back from my oil canvas and tried to eye the painting with a fresh, unbiased perspective. I'd already blocked in the background colors for my portrait, soft hues of green and blue that complemented the model's flowing peach dress.

Maiko sat facing us, her long hair a rich brown-black that draped across her shoulder like a dark river. Her perfect skin was creamy, pale with blushing undertones, and her small hands rested on her lap. She was a great model, motionless but somehow still filled with life, drawing our attention to her naturally.

I'd totally captured the gentle emotion on her face, the relaxed lines of her body. But I wasn't pleased with the tones I'd mixed for her hair. They didn't feel . . . warm enough, somehow. What was I doing wrong? A bubble of frustration welled in me.

"Coming along great, Corinne," Teni Achebe, the local artist-in-residence who ran our summer workshop, said as she slipped behind me. She studied my painting, head tilted, taking in everything.

I suddenly felt like she could see every flaw, and I fought the urge to cover the whole thing with my hands. "I don't know what I'm messing up about her hair," I finally confessed, my face flushed hot. I rubbed the back of my neck with my clean hand. "It's falling flat for me."

"Hmm. Take a close look at the shades in her hair," she instructed, pointing me toward Maiko, who sat serenely, staring off into space. "You have the browns and blacks, but do you see a hint of red, too? That's the warm tone your painting is missing."

Wow. Now that she pointed it out, I could see a touch of red where the soft light hit the crown of her hair. How had I missed that?

"Thank you," I said, pouring appreciation into my voice.

"Just a thin layer over what you've already painted. Make it light, almost transparent, and I think you'll see that warmth you desire pop right out." She smiled at me, her dark brown eyes crinkling in the corners.

Teni, a tall slender African woman, was in her forties, with only a few hints of gray threading through her many braids. She wore gold bangle bracelets, her dress bearing an abstract batik pattern in bright red, green, and purple. Teni had moved to Ohio from Nigeria as a young girl and had worked in retail for a number of years, but her art had exploded a few years ago when she'd been featured in a New York gallery opening. Her five paintings had sold within a few hours for jaw-dropping prices, and things had gone uphill for her ever since.

Last year Teni had opened a summer residency program for local Cleveland area high schoolers, grades ten through twelve, who were interested in seriously studying art under her tutelage. I'd spent much of my tenth grade year waiting in nervous anticipation to see if I'd made the list. When I'd finally gotten the call from her right before the school year ended, I'd squealed for about an hour.

"Keep up the good work," Teni said with a smile as she moved on to the guy at the easel beside me. He looked up at her in desperate hope as she leaned closer and started whispering tips on how to make the face more realistic.

I turned my attention back to my painting, created the thin red wash, and layered it over her hair. It was a subtle touch, but it made all the difference. I couldn't fight the smile that crept over my face. After a few more minutes of fussing with minor details, I paused and put my brush down. I needed a small brain break.

Curiosity finally overtook me, and I scanned the rest of the room to see how everyone else's projects were going. Being in the middle of the room, I was able to check out a number of other students' artwork. Our studio was roomy but not too big, with a dozen stations spread throughout.

Sunlight poured in from rows of large windows, sending rays across our art—Teni had insisted from day one that the key to amazing art was good lighting, no matter what your media was. So she kept all the blinds open every class. Fortunately, she also kept the air-conditioning kicked on to prevent the room from getting overly hot.

There were a couple of people scattered around who were doing classical oil paintings like me. I saw a guy working with watercolor as he painted Maiko's hair. One of the girls near the front was doing her piece entirely in pen; she painstakingly drew hatch marks for shading and created 3-D tones that awed me.

I had to admit—her artwork looked fabulous from where I was standing. She'd captured Maiko's almond-shaped eyes and high cheekbones, the twinkle of life in her irises, despite it all being black and grayscale. Maybe I needed to work on deepening my darker tones.

My attention then caught on the tall guy standing beside her, wearing long black shorts and a plain white T-shirt. His brown hair was tousled, as if he'd run his hands through it multiple times. Matthew Bonder—he attended my school and had also just finished his sophomore year, a basketball player who generally hung out with a bunch of jocks. I bit back an irritated sigh and looked at his . . . painting, I guess you could call it. It was very postmodern, with strokes of abstract black lines I supposed were meant to represent the model's form. I could hardly find a face on the page.

I knew it was kind of snobby to think so, but that just wasn't real art for me. I liked actually being able to discern features, to see the meticulous effort of re-creating life around us. Abstract stuff was confusing—it felt like the artist was trying to pass off something that had taken all of five minutes to create.

How had he even gotten into this class?

I think I'd talked to Matthew a total of five seconds our entire freshman and sophomore years. Needless to say, we ran in different circles. I was captain of the mathlete team, president of our school's French club. My friends and I didn't really hang at any sporting events except for the occasional football game. It took a lot of academic focus to maintain my 4.0 GPA, but I did it.

Matthew, on the other hand, had sat in the back row of our few shared classes, barely speaking a word. Who even knew what grades he was making? From what I could tell, he funneled all of his discernible attention into sports—basketball, baseball, golf. I'd never seen him show any interest in art, so it had floored me when I'd walked in the door a couple of weeks ago and there he was.

As if he could sense my thoughts, Matthew looked over his shoulder and locked eyes with me. My face burned from getting caught staring at him and his work, and I swallowed. He simply raised an eyebrow and gave the smallest shadow of a smile, his dark blue eyes sparkling just a touch.

I tore my gaze away and fixed my eyes firmly back on my own painting. Crud. That was awkward.

The rest of the class session went pretty fast. I worked on adding small details to my painting—her fingernails, the thin brows above her eyes, the lace on the bottom of her dress. I was almost done with my piece, which was good; we'd been working on this particular project, our first as a group, for a solid couple of weeks now.

What would be our next big class project? I was excited to move on and do something new and challenging.

"Wow. I'm so proud of your progress," Teni said as she moved to the front of the room. Her dress swirled around her slender legs, and she propped a hand on Maiko's shoulder, giving her a grateful smile. "Before class ends for the day, I wanted to discuss an opportunity I think a few of you might be interested in."

Opportunity? I found myself perking up. I put down my paintbrush and gave her my full attention.

"Every year there's a nationwide art competition, with artists like myself sponsoring promising high school students to enter. It's hard work—you *really* have to push yourself beyond what you think you're capable of, because you're competing with the entire United States."

There was a collective "ooh" from the class. My stomach tightened in anticipation. I knew right then that whatever it was, I wanted in. Nothing excited me more than a good challenge, and growing in my art craft would be a bonus.

"This year's competition is. . . ." She paused, gave a smile. "Well, it's unique. But I have a feeling my students will rise to the occasion. The prize is five thousand dollars, plus an all-expenses-paid trip for you and your family to New York City to see your artwork on display in a real gallery at a notable exhibition. Plus, that artwork will be featured in a full-page spread in a national magazine—and I can't say which one yet, because that's still in the works and nothing is finalized. But you've all heard of it, I'm sure." She winked.

I was fairly certain my heart stopped beating for a moment. All the blood rushed to my ears, and when my pulse finally kick-started again, it roared in my head.

Wow. That was a huge prize.

"Miss Achebe," the line-drawing girl in the front said, raising her hand, "when does the competition take place? And how do we enter?"

"I'm getting right to that, Natalia," she said with a smile. She turned her attention to all of us. "I spent these first couple of weeks here evaluating your art, getting a sense of who you all are. What skills you have and how you need to grow. I firmly believe any of you would do a fantastic job in the competition. But the timeline is very short." Her face turned serious. "I need you to present to me your best work of art, the one that most represents your style and technique, by Friday after class. The judging for the competition will take place just over a month from now."

There were a couple of dismayed gasps.

Teni held up her hands. "Look, I know that is a very short turnaround, but if you want it badly enough, you can do it. You have a few days to either find a piece in your oeuvre or create something new. And it can't be the piece you used to get into this workshop," she added with a regretful smile. "I've already seen that one. Push yourselves to dig deep and wow me. I'm only going to sponsor the best, because it's a time and money investment for me. But I know it'll be worth it."

I scrabbled through my memory to see if I had anything in my room, in my portfolio that might work. There were a few pictures I'd drawn—but of course, my best piece I'd already used to get into this class.

No, I would just have to create something new. But what?

"If you have any questions for me, I'm available to talk more after class. For now, go ahead and use the remaining time to finish your work for the day and clean up your stations."

The guy beside me muttered, "No way I'd be ready in time. I barely got into this class to begin with. Are you gonna enter?"

I nodded. "Not sure what I'm going to paint though. I'm not quite satisfied with the stuff I already have."

He gave me a big grin, picked up his brush—loaded with acrylic paint—and rinsed it. He was gawky, with a shock of black hair and thick brows, and wore trendy horn-rimmed glasses. His smile was friendly. "Well, good luck. I think you'll do a great job." He nodded toward my painting. "That looks amazing. Just like her."

"Thanks." With dismay, I realized I'd never introduced myself to him. "I'm Corrine, by the way."

"Henry." He stuck out a hand and shook mine. "I go to Berea High School—I'm going to be a senior. You?"

"I'm here in Lakewood," I said. "I'll be a junior." Wow, it still felt great to say that.

"Nice to finally 'meet' you." He finished rinsing his brushes in his small cup and took his palette to the washing station in the corner, where there were several big sinks.

I used turpentine to clean the oil paint off my brushes, straightened my station, and gingerly stepped around my painting, not wanting to disturb the still-wet paint. I ran smack into a tall, lean chest. "Oh, sorry," I said, holding up a hand and stepping back.

Matthew peered down at me, one side of his mouth upturned. "No, I'm sorry. I was just barreling right through here."

I gave a tight smile and moved past him to toss my paper towels. Then I told Teni I'd see her on Wednesday, grabbed my backpack, and headed out the door, stepping into the hot sunshine. June in Cleveland could be surprisingly humid, and we were in a particularly dry spell right now.

I was extra fortunate that the art workshop was only a mile away from my house, so I hoofed it down the sidewalk blocks here in Lakewood, past small consignment shops and mom-and-pop diners. I loved the vibe of this neighborhood—the eclectic mix of people, the art galleries and jewelry stores scattered around. The sun beat down on the back of my neck, and sweat dribbled along my collar, sliding down my spine. Wow, it was a warm one today.

I turned my focus back to the issue at hand. What art project was I going to do? The pressure wrapped itself around my chest, squeezing my lungs. I was excited—and petrified. Maybe Grandpa could give me some ideas. Yeah, I wasn't going to be helping at the bakery until Saturday, but maybe I could give him a call.

Grandpa was a bit of an artist himself, though his focus was on food. He'd opened the bakery about thirty years ago, and it had grown into a staple in our neighborhood. His cakes were to die for—rich, decadent, with decorations that blew my mind. As much as I loved painting and drawing, somehow I could never get the hang of using those little frosting bags. My work always turned out too lumpy.

He would take the bag from me with a laugh and fix the mistakes, making them look like they were intentional. I was in awe of his skills.

I let my gaze wander around the neighborhood, watched kids playing on the street, drawing with hot-pink chalk and giggling. One little girl had fat braids on both sides of her head. Her skin tone matched mine, a dark brown with golden undertones. Reminded me of when I was a kid, sitting with my younger brother at the park, both of us wearing brightly colored outfits and posing for Mom's camera.

I stopped in place. That would be fun—maybe I could paint a picture from a photograph of when I was younger. It would certainly challenge me. And my mom had hundreds of pictures in her albums. Surely I could find one that would work. I could paint it in acrylics or watercolor so it would dry in time. Not as challenging as oil painting, but either medium still gave me the ability to make something worthwhile.

My heart fluttered. This was going to happen. A chance for me to do something big. Yes, I'd had a lot of accomplishments in my life, things I was proud of. Academic achievements that I'd worked hard for. But nothing would compare to winning a nationwide art contest.

Being in a gallery. In New York City.

The stakes were high, and from looking at the artwork of several of the fellow artists in my room, the competition was stiff. But I had to make this work. I'd spend all my free time working on this piece.

I wasn't going to fail. I would put my heart and soul into it, and pray, pray, pray that it was good enough for me to qualify.